Better is Ahead

Better is Ahead

You were born for a life of success

Dr Simon Wallace

Published by Simon Wallace
Contact: swallace@newdayministries.co.uk

Dedication

I dedicate this book to:

My Heavenly Father
Who says, "I am fearfully and wonderfully made."

My Loving Parents
Dr C T Wallace and Mother E I Wallace.
Although you may be laid up now and can't get around like before,
You still both inspire me very much.

My Family
My lovely wife, Brenda. We are so much better together.
My three sons: Andre, Anton and Jaden.
Don't ever stop dreaming; keep pushing forward.
You can achieve anything in life.

My Church
(NewDay Ministries Christian Centre)
I've been blessed to pastor the most incredible church.
I've watched you grow both spiritually and numerically.
I love every last one of you.
Thank you for faithfully showing up every week.

About the Author

Dr Simon Wallace is a graduate of Canada Christian College and the European Theological Seminary. As an inspired pastor, speaker and author, he is known for his practical dynamic teaching with a passionate delivery as a motivator and exhorter. He has an encouraging message that cuts across denominational and cultural barriers. As Senior Pastor of NewDay Ministries Christian Centre, he is a visionary who believes it is God's will for you to prosper and be in health and is committed to helping educate people to what God's Word has to say about them.

Born and raised in the southeast of London from an early age, he excelled within the area of music. After forming two of the country's most outstanding community choirs, he toured several countries as an accomplished musician. He received awards for being both a prolific songwriter and one of the pioneers of gospel music in the UK. His God-given anointing and talents made him one of the most sought-after gospel artists of the 90s.

At the age of forty, Simon received a call to start NewDay Ministries Christian Centre. After following the Holy Spirit's leading, what began as a seed grew and flourished into this incredible, powerful, life-changing ministry that exists today. Simon has been given a unique anointing and a relevant message that has opened doors for him to minister in the UK, USA and the Caribbean. Among the many hats worn by Simon, he is also a pastor, mentor, husband and father. Still, at the very core, he is a worshiper and seeks to help people encounter God through inspired worship and relevant application of the Word of God in their daily lives.

Table of Contents

Introduction

"Some wake up to an alarm. Others wake up to a calling."

Life can be chaotic and puzzling. In its mysterious way, it comes at you at a relentless speed, similar to a jet speeding down a runway, expecting you to be able to decipher and deal with whatever it drags along with it—often leaving us confused as to what to do next.

Have you ever been there? Have you ever wondered, is this it? Is this the sum-total of what my life is going to be? Or perhaps you're that person who is just starting out, embarking upon a new career, starting that new business, beginning a new relationship, and you're wondering, is this going to be all that I dreamed it would be.

The good news is, no longer do you have to be afraid, worried or apprehensive about any of these decisions. Better is ahead, and this book takes you on an exciting and engaging journey from ordinary to better. It speaks to everyday spiritual struggles, questions and longings of the human soul. It inspires and encourages anyone who has ever struggled to break free from the grip of limitation, enabling them to walk in the power and freedom of the better life that is rightfully theirs. It is the kind of life we all should be experiencing.

Ivan Pavlov once quoted, "If you want a new idea, read an old book." This exciting new book that you are holding in your hands points to the greatest book ever written, extrapolating the biblical truths, making one aware of the better covenant we have now been given along with its better promises. It cleverly crosses over generations, careers and callings, pushing you to run when you can, walk when you have to, crawl if you must, but never to give up.

It carefully explains why so many of us have not yet experienced living the better life that is rightfully ours, and it gives instructions on how we can obtain this and live life to the full.

Reading this book is the first step to discovering how to live a better life. Romans 8:30–32 says, 'Whom he predestined, those he also called. Whom he called, those he also justified. Whom he justified, those he also glorified. What then shall we say about these things? If God is for us, who can be against us?"

So, as you can see, not only were you born for this, you were called for this. "Some wake up to an alarm. Others wake up to a calling" let's wake up to it and embrace it together through the pages of this book.

"There once was a very cautious man,
who never laughed or cried,
he never cared, he never dared
he never dreamed or tried.
And when one day he passed away,
his insurance was denied,
for since he never really lived
they claimed he never died."

Author unknown

1

There Is Still Time

This Book of the Law shall not depart from your mouth, but you shall meditate on it day and night, so that you may be careful to do according to all that is written in it. For then you will make your way prosperous, and then you will have good success.

(Joshua 1:8)

What is success? What does it look like? Many people have tried to answer these questions with various approaches, but the necessary key that unlocks the door with the correct answer resides in yet another question, and that is, who defines it? Who decides what real success is? To the world, success is reaching an objective, completing a goal, achieving some sort of social status that goes along with the achievement; whilst God's definition of success is vastly different. The world sees it as achieving something useful for this life alone; God sees success as something that is useful for this life and yet has eternal, infinite value for life to come. So, the Bible portrays success in a different way than that of the world. In fact, the Bible makes a distinction between success and good success, which is comparable to having life and having abundant life.

Most people aspire to become successful in their chosen field, personal interest or by using their innate gift, even if it is not for now but at some point or time further down the road. I can now say, like David, "I've been young, and now I'm old," and I have never seen or met anybody who is simply content with being unsuccessful in life.

> *"I spent my whole life climbing the wall of success only to reach the top and find out my ladder was leaning against the wrong wall."*
>
> JEB MCGRUDER

Being unsuccessful has never been somebody's lifetime goal or desire; although it is possible to drift into this indifference after a lifetime of failure, nobody starts out with a desire to be unsuccessful in anything because it is not in their DNA.

Everyone is looking for success, but sadly many seek it in the wrong places. Some think they can find it through the lottery, and so they rush out every week to buy a ticket. Others download the latest betting app and put money down on a horse or a game. Others invest in pyramid schemes or the latest get-rich-quick schemes, all seeking some kind of success. However, good success, which is the kind that last, begins with the Word of God.

The command to be successful was first given to Adam when God blessed him and told him to "Be fruitful and multiply and fill the earth and subdue it, and have dominion over the fish of the sea and over the birds of the heavens and over every living thing that moves on the earth." (Gen. 1:28). In that command given to Adam,

God was speaking to every one of us, to have dominion, to rule over our area of influence, but it feels like a crisis when the success we seek seems to be eluding us. We experience inner turmoil that we struggle to articulate.

When the word crisis is mentioned, far too often our minds race immediately towards things that can be measured and seen by the natural eye. For example, we look at disturbances in nature or our environment that cause significant change and call it a biological crisis. Similarly, when the business world is hit financially, we accept that to be a financial crisis. Even with the wrongful human application of science and technology, which causes a breakdown in our technology, we call it a technological crisis. A myriad of examples can be brought forward to show exactly what the dictionary describes a crisis to be. One thing for sure is that a crisis can be described briefly as a time of intense difficulty or danger. However, a crisis is not always an external dilemma; some of the most painful crises exist internally. One type that is too often overlooked is the pain that comes from a crisis called the identity crisis.

Identity Crisis

In psychology, an Identity Crisis is defined as "the failure to achieve ego identity during adolescence." It's a time of intensive analysis and exploration of different ways of looking at oneself. The German Theorist, Erik Erikson, who is best known for his famous theory of psychosocial development, coined the phrase Identity Crisis. He believed that it was one of the most important conflicts people face in development. Most of us have had a stage in our adolescence where we wanted to find who we are and what we were going to be. We had a deep belief and a confident hope that greatness was out there awaiting us in our not-too-distant future.

Erick H. Erikson once said, "Hope is both the earliest and the most indispensable virtue inherent in the state of being alive." If life is to be sustained, hope must remain, even where confidence is wounded. The writer of Hebrews spoke about the power of hope when he wrote, "Faith is the substance of things hoped for the evidence of things not seen" (Heb.11:1). Hope is then an essential virtue if we are to overcome an Identity Crisis, discover who we are and walk into our purpose. Success is awaiting us.

Midlife Crises

Hope deferred maketh the heart sick:
but when the desire cometh, it is a tree of life.

(Prov. 13:12 KJV)

We all have expectations for life, dreams and aspirations; for some, it is to get married and have children; for others, it is to achieve a certain level of riches in life and have a successful career and ultimately live a long and happy life. Sometimes those dreams are realised as planned and come very quickly, but most of the time, they do not. And when our dreams, our aspirations, and our expectations are delayed, and things are not going the way we envisaged, then the reality of life and real-life storms begin to beat against our hopes, dreams, and expectations. When life does this on a consistent basis, disillusionment and the storm clouds of discouragement begin to weigh heavy on us. And if we are not careful, they will begin to suffocate us even though we once believed and had hope of a better life.

That's why as soon as that thirty-ninth birthday becomes visible in the rear-view mirror, some of us have been known to question ourselves, analyse our lives and some sink into a depression and although some of us struggle to articulate exactly what it is, we are feeling, those who have experienced it and come out the other end can look back at it and call it exactly what it is - A Midlife Crisis.

> "Don't try to rush progress. Remember a step forward, no matter how small, is a step in the right direction. Keep believing."
>
> KARA GOUCHER

Psychologists use the term "Midlife Crisis" to describe a transitional stage in adult development. During this period of time, men and women have been known to behave quite differently. A woman may feel the need to reinvent herself, buy a new wardrobe, and even a new face. At this same stage, men have been known to buy sports cars and go off with a new girlfriend half their age. It is described as that midway time between adulthood and the end of life when people naturally struggle with questions about their unique purpose; once again when success seems to elude them.

This can be exacerbated when our plans and goals in life are delayed or disrupted. There are very few things that are worse than the feeling that you are running out of time to do what you want to do. That moment when we first become aware that life is passing us by, those of us who have made dissatisfying life choices feel especially troubled as we realize there is a finite amount of time left. When we reflect and see our goals unattained, risks not taken, and bucket lists unmet, sadness, doubt, and even anger can arise. Then there is often a wish to return to one's youth or do life over, but no one can reverse the time; try as you may. You can undergo plastic surgery to turn the clock back on how you look; it still will not add another inch or minute to your time. What we must do is keep hope alive, and although our hope has been deferred, it is not denied. That thing that God has put in your heart will come to pass. Better is ahead.

Universal Hope

"Patience is the red carpet upon which God's grace approaches us."

We see throughout many historical writing accounts men and women whose hopes and dreams faded with time. As humans and especially Christians, we must learn to live with deferred hope without allowing our hearts to get sick.

Many have experienced a time when the heart is sad, but God created the mind with the capacity to accept and cope with the hope that is deferred and yet still go on in life with enthusiasm. But this is a mindset that one must adopt and walk with.

When I look at all those in the Bible who received a promise from God, none of them received the fulfilment straight away. From Genesis to Revelation, we see (Promise - A period of time -

Fulfilment). Abraham was given a promise that he was going to be the father of many nations, making his wife Sarah the mother of many nations. This was an exciting promise, seeing that Sarah was childless and barren. Up until now, Sarah's barrenness felt like a curse. Most of the other women in her life were fertile and productive, and when it seemed like all hope was gone of having a child, God shows up with a promise, a promise so far-fetched that when Sarah heard it, she laughed.

It was a laugh of disbelief; after all, how can an old woman fall pregnant after menopause? It all seemed utterly impossible. Abraham and Sarah were promised a child, then had to wait 25 years before Isaac was even felt moving in her womb. It is in those lonely times of waiting when hope is deferred that the heart feels sick, but when the promise comes, it is a tree of life.

> "Never doubt in the dark what God told you in the light."
>
> V. RAYMOND EDMAN

David was but a teenager when he was anointed to be king. It wasn't going to come easy; promises rarely do. We are told in (1 Sam. 16) that Jesse made his seven sons go before the prophet Samuel one-by-one, but none of those sons were God's choice for who He wanted to be king over Israel. All of these sons looked like kings with their strong physical appearances, but none of them had the heart God was looking for. God was looking for a man after His own heart.

After Jessie's seven sons passed before Samuel the prophet, Samuel asked Jessie if he had another son because Samuel was told by God that a king would come out of Jessie's house. Only after being asked this question did Jessie admit to having another son who was currently outside looking after the sheep. When David eventually came into the house, Samuel took the horn of oil and anointed David in the midst of his brothers, and the Spirit of the Lord came mightily upon David.

Samuel anointed David as king at the early age of seventeen, but David would have to wait until he was thirty before he would wear the crown and be placed in the position as King. I'm sure many days passed with him wondering, "Is this really going to happen? Will I ever wear the crown?" But with God, timing is important. Nothing is done before the time. God knows exactly when to fulfil the promise he has made to you, and when he does, it will not be a moment too late. David did become king, and the most successful King Israel ever had.

Hannah was another faithful and godly woman of Judah who lamented the fact that she could not bear children (1 Samuel 1:5-7). Peninnah, her husband's other wife, had sons and daughters and, in time, began to make life "bitter" for Hannah with her constant teasing. Hannah was often in tears and broken-hearted because of her fading hope of ever bringing a child into the world. She sorrowfully prayed to God not once or twice but on many occasions, then through a prophet of God, a promise was given to her that she would bear a child, and all of a sudden, hope was rekindled. And when the time was right (And only when the time was right), God blessed her with a son who would become the greatest prophet of his time.

In each of these examples, all of them received a promise and then had to wait a substantial period of time before they walked in their promise. This, my friend, is a part of life when we walk with God. Those dreams God gave you, those promises God made to you, those aspirations God placed in you are all for an appointed time, Habakkuk reminds us, "For the vision is yet for an appointed time, but at the end, it shall speak, and not lie: though it tarries, wait for it; because it will surely come, it will not tarry" (Hab. 2:3 KJV). You will see success; success has been given your name.

Speaking of tarrying and waiting, allow me to now bring forward at least one example from the New Testament as all the above examples were from the Old. After telling his disciples that he would have to leave them, Jesus also promised his disciples that after his death, resurrection and ascension, he would send the Holy Spirit. He was adamant that the disciples should not go and pursue ministry until they receive the power from the Holy Spirit. The exact instruction was to go to Jerusalem and wait in the upper room.

When you read the account in Acts chapter one, it tells us there were one hundred and twenty believers gathered waiting on the promise. Which means for fifty days, they were waiting and worshipping. For fifty days, they were cooped up in a room with one hundred and twenty people, that could not have been easy for any of them, but they were instructed to wait before they would ever receive what was promised. Can you imagine the wait? Some of us would have left because we want everything now, we are accustomed to having things come quickly, but as they say, "Anything worth having, is worth waiting for," and there is a famous saying "Good things come to those that wait," this is especially true when we are referring to waiting on the Lord.

These disciples had no idea they would have to wait in those conditions for fifty days but thank God they did. The Bible states, "When the day of Pentecost came, they were all together in one place. Suddenly a sound like the blowing of a violent wind came from heaven and filled the whole house where they were sitting. They saw what seemed to be tongues of fire that came and rested on each of them. All of them were filled with the Holy Spirit and began to speak in other tongues as the Spirit enabled them" (Acts 2:1-4 NIV).

Do you see what they could have missed out on had they been impatient and decided not to wait? Waiting is a virtue and a blessing when done with the right attitude. God always rewards it with something big. "But those who wait upon God get fresh strength. They spread their wings and soar like eagles, they run and don't get tired, they walk and don't lag behind" (Isaiah 40:31 MSG). Teach us Lord, how to wait.

So, to the person that is holding this book, I am so excited for you, believe me when I tell you - Better is ahead of you. I see you in the future, and you look so much better than you do right now.

"You are who you are for a reason,
You're part of an intricate plan.
You're a precious and perfect unique design,
Called God's special woman or man

You look like you look for reason
Our God made no mistake
He knit you together within the womb
You're just what he wanted to make

The parents you had were the ones he chose,
And no matter how you may feel
They were custom designed with God's plan in mind
And they bear the Masters' seal.

No, that trauma you faced was not easy,
And God wept that it hurt you so;
But it was allowed to shape your heart
So that into his likeness you'd grow.

You are who you are for a reason
You've been formed by the Master's rod
You are who you are, beloved,
Because there is a God!"

Russell Kelfer

*"If people are doubting how far you can go,
go so far that you can't hear them anymore."*

MICHELE RUIZ

2

From Potential to Purpose

"I see you in the future and you look so much better than you do right now"

When we sit together to have a conversation regarding purpose, our conversation cannot start with anyone else but "Yahweh" God, our creator. God must be our starting point. For it is in Him that we live, move and have our being (Acts 17:28 KJV). Contrary to what you may have heard in seminars or may have read in books, before your parents conceived you, you were conceived in the mind of God. That being said, you were no accident; you were not an afterthought, God wanted you here, and your coming here was by divine design.

However, when God created you, He gave you free will to choose your hobbies, career, spouse, and other parts of your life but not your purpose because your purpose fits into a much larger cosmic purpose that God has designed for eternity. His purpose for your life was decided long ago, predating your conception. He decided it without your input. He assigned it without your consultation and placed it without your knowledge. God has a divine plan for your life.

This awareness that you are here, by divine design, should excite you and fill you with much confidence. The knowledge alone of God deciding what race you would be a part of, what skin you would wear, what nationality you would have, the personality you would be given, and all the talents you would possess should assure you that you are uniquely created with a purpose in mind.

David reminds us of this, listen to what he says, "You know every bone in my body; You know exactly how I was made, bit by bit, how I was sculpted from nothing into something. Like an open book, you watched me grow from conception to birth; all the stages of my life were spread out before you, the days of my life all prepared before I'd even lived one day" (Psalms 139:15 MSG). Since God created us with purpose in mind, the discovering and the fulfilling of our purpose must take precedence over everything else.

The discovery of potential

Not too long ago I gave myself a simple exercise to do, I told myself to look outside the window and just within the scope of that window to describe everything I could see. At first, I could easily describe the glaringly obvious. It was easy to notice the large objects. I noticed the houses across the way, the colours of the paintwork on the wood trimmings. I noticed the designs of brickwork including the colour of the cement that held the bricks together. I noticed the greenery and the different types of plants in the front gardens. I also noticed other things I would normally take for granted, but the longer I kept looking the more I noticed, and every time I thought I was done, I would see something else that I did not see before. I marvelled that even after a prolonged time of observing, I still couldn't describe everything I was seeing, because there was always more detail that I had overlooked.

Packed with promise

By the same token, If I were to ask you to look out into your garden and describe to me what you see, you might say to me, I see different trees and plants, flowers and blades of grass, animals and birds, but in truth, that's not all you would be seeing, because within each of those trees are seeds for more trees. Within each of those plants are seeds for more plants; within each insect and animal resides the potential for more insect and animals to be birthed. Likewise, if I held a cherry seed in my hand, even though it may appear to be singular and solitary, in reality, I am holding much more than a single seed because within that seed, there's a tree, and from that tree would spring yet other trees with yet more cherries.

"The abortion of potential is the death of the future."

I have said all of this and laboured this point to show you what untapped potential looks like. God created the earth and everything in it to be able to reproduce after its own kind. He infused it with potential. By definition, 'potential' is defined as

15

"having or showing the capacity to develop into something in the future." It describes "What can be". God, our creator, did that. He also planted within us the ability to do and be much more than we are right now.

Ponder this for a moment, as human beings and particularly believers, when we are not growing and developing into what God sees that we can be, it is as though the potential that God invested in us is being untapped and wasted. This unexposed ability, this capped capability, this dormant success simply lays within us, not wanting to be ignored, suffocated or destroyed but released.

There is one thing, however, I must bring to your attention regarding this, and that is the need of guarding and protecting your potential. Being blessed in having a large garden to take care of has taught me a valuable lesson about potential. Every year I am reminded and amazed at how quickly unwanted weeds seem to grow. To have a garden with little to no weeds requires that you put in much work in cultivating it. Weeds grow much faster than anything else in the garden, and if left unchecked, they will quickly smother and choke other precious tender shoots. Therefore, cultivation becomes essential if you hope to produce vegetation and enjoy a beautiful, productive garden.

I have discovered that when dealing with the seed of potential, cultivation is just as important. Carefully protecting and removing from it negative influences that could choke or stunt its growth is essential. I hesitate to say that there may be some people who need to be uprooted from your life; those who mean you no good and those who always have something negative to say. The Bible instructs, "Death and life are in the power of the tongue" (Prov.18:

2 KJV). It is harder to reach for the stars when somebody is constantly telling you that, "Nobody has ever done that before." One of the biggest negative influences on potential can be family or friends, although they mean well.

We learn from Scripture that Satan has a three-fold purpose - to kill, steal and destroy; you'd be surprised to learn that often times he will use people to accomplish his objective. That spark of potential that resides in you, he wants to kill, before it gets a chance to grow into what it can be. So, the release of your potential has much to do with how you are able to protect it. Those plans and your imaginations must be protected. Those big dreams must be kept far away from small dreamers so that when the time is right, they can blossom into what they must be, but always bear in mind, the devil has much experience in trying to destroy the seed.

When the serpent caused Adam and Eve to sin in the Garden of Eden, God said to the serpent, "And I will put enmity between you and the woman, and between your seed and her Seed; He shall bruise your head, and you shall bruise His heel" (Gen. 3:15 KJV). This Scripture is referred to as the (Protoevangelium) which is the first mention of the coming of Christ.

The devil did not quite know who the Seed would be, and so as early as when Moses - the first deliverer for Israel - was born, the devil tried to kill him, thinking he was the Seed. You read in Exodus 1:15-16 that Pharaoh instructed the Hebrew midwives that if a male child was born, to kill him. This genocide was an attempt to kill the Seed of the woman, but Jochebed was not the woman, and Moses was not the Seed. Later, King Herod tried to do the same at the birth of Jesus. He initiated the murder of all the infants in

Bethlehem in an attempt to get rid of Jesus, this was once again the devil trying to get rid of the Seed, but he failed. Mary was the woman, and Jesus was the Seed.

Potential can be likened to a baby in a womb fighting to come out; it just won't keep still because it has work to do. Think for a moment about all that takes place in the biological development and growth of a human being. In order to go from conception to full maturity, firstly, a seed of an adult male has to come in contact with an egg from an adult female; once fused together, it can be fertilised. After the fertilisation process, the egg grows and develops into an embryo and then a foetus. When the foetal stage is complete - normally nine months - a beautiful new-born baby enters the world. That baby then begins to develop outside the womb within his new environment, and within just a few years, he develops into a toddler, after a few more years into childhood, adolescence and later adulthood. It all happens at the right time in the right sequence of events.

> "Potential is a priceless treasure like gold. All of us have it hidden within but we have to dig to get it out."
>
> ANONYMOS

As you can see, with God everything starts with a seed. He designed it that way. You may pray for an oak tree, and God gives you an acorn seed, and if you're not careful, you'll dismiss God's gift of the acorn, not realising that what God has given you has the potential to grow into the oak tree you were asking for. God gave you just what you needed, but in seed form, because God is always after your development.

Even Jesus is referred to in scripture as a Seed, and when we accept Him into our life, all the other blessings, such as joy and peace, come into our spirit in seed form too. Seeds develop and become what they are destined to become.

Going back to my illustration - Once a foetus is passed through the birth canal and experiences the natural process of being birthed, it is no longer a foetus, and it is no longer a seed. No one that is birthed into this world ever continued to exist in seed form. Each of us became something greater; we grew into the full maturity of our potential. The process of "Becoming" is always expected. Growth and development are natural processes.

Noah Webster's 1828 American Dictionary of the English language defines potential as "Existing in possibility, not in act." I particularly like this definition because it places emphasis on the necessity of form. Somebody once compared it to concrete, needing something to pour into, something to give it shape and make it useful. Without form, it abides alone. This is what Jesus explained in John 12:24 when he said, "Truly, truly, I say to you, unless a grain of wheat falls into the earth and dies, it remains alone; but if it dies, it bears much fruit."

Potential in the right form creates an environment where it can take shape, thrive and prosper. A receptive mind is a perfect place in which potential needs to be poured because that is where your decisions are made. Once you recognise your potential and make a faith-based decision to use it, it will surely bring forth fruit in your life and lead you into purpose.

This undeveloped potential exists in all of us, and the danger is that we will never see it manifest until we accept and believe that we can do everything God said we can do in his word. ".... Greater things you will do because I am going to my father" (Jn 14:12 KJV). Unless we are willing to step out in faith with the assurance that "with God nothing is impossible," our potential will never be developed.

Purpose

And let us not grow weary of doing good,
for in due season we will reap, if we do not give up.

(Gal.6:9 NIV)

Potential developed leads into purpose. This is where faith is essential. Potential demands faith, and faith makes demands of potential. Faith is the catalyst that makes things happen. It is the substance of what you hope for. It makes you move in a realm where you may not be able to see with your physical eyes where you are going, but as we continue to walk by faith and not by sight, whilst trusting God, you will be led right into purpose.

Olympic runner Eric Liddell in the movie Chariots of Fire said, "I believe God made me for a purpose, and he also made me fast, and when I run, I feel God's pleasure." I believe when we walk in our purpose, God smiles down on us because we are fulfilling our potential.

God gives us the potential to push us into purpose. Purpose is a powerful thing; without it, life has no meaning. Solomon says, "Many are the plans in a man's heart, but it is the purpose of the Lord that shall prevail" (Pr. 19: 21 KJV). God's purpose for your life is more important than your plans for your life. And the wonderful thing about going from potential to purpose is the knowledge that no matter what negative thing happens, everything is still going to work out in your favour because "all things work together for good not only to them that love the Lord but to them that are the called according to purpose" (Rom. 8:28 KJV).

This Scripture really resonates with me because it forms the crux of my testimony. It was never my intention to go into pastoral work; my plans were far removed from this. My dream was to become a musician and tour the world. I excelled in music and thought that was going to be my fulfilment. I spent much of my early years pursuing music and was quite successful. I founded and directed two of the country's greatest choirs. I excelled in playing many musical instruments. I toured various countries and appeared on various TV and radio shows doing what I loved, but God had a purpose in mind for me, which I submitted myself to. Much of my giftings and experiences is utilised now that I am walking in purpose.

When one walks in purpose, not only do they see the personal fruit, but they see others getting into position too, because your purpose is a part of God's bigger cosmic purpose, and like a jigsaw puzzle, the bigger cosmic plan of God requires the pieces to be in place. I've seen this and continue to see it in my church family. The lives that have been changed and affected constantly astounds me. The awesome testimonies we hear every Sunday of what God is doing in people's lives amazes me. I sometimes wonder what would have happened to all these souls if I had refused to walk in my purpose.

I remember preaching at a christening held at my church one Sunday morning, and after service, a visitor and her family walked up to the front and said to me, "You don't know how much you have changed our lives. We have been looking for a church for such a long time, but we just couldn't find the right one." I thought to myself, but there are many churches out there, and you passed many to get here, I had no idea what she meant, but she did. I thanked God that I could be in the place where He could use me to affect the life of another person like that.

Purpose guarantees you a God-ordained success, and the more you tap into purpose, the more successful you are going to be. Your prosperity, fulfilment and peace are found in your purpose because purpose produces contentment. You do not have to be jealous of anybody when you're walking in your God-ordained purpose because what God is leading you to do, is different from where he is leading others. It stops you from being tempted to compare yourself and your successes with anybody else's. Purpose is liberating; anything we do outside of our purpose becomes a huge waste of time.

I once heard the story of a young man who found a vein of gold in a mountain. He wanted to get it out himself but did not know how to. He went into town and asked a mining company to come to take a look at it. The mining company surveyed the mountain and the vein of gold and wanted to buy it. They offered him a large amount of cash if he would sell it to them.

The young man considered it then decided that rather than selling it to the mining company, he would learn all he could learn about mining. Over the next year, he studied practically all the time; he read every book on mining he could find and spoke to every person who would give him any information about it. He devoted all his attention to learning how to mine gold. At the end of the year, he went back to the mountain and began to dig out the gold. It was hard work, but in the end, he had millions and millions to show for it.

The story is a valuable lesson because when he saw the vein of gold in the mountain, he saw potential, but for it to be developed, it had to become his purpose. He purposed in his heart that no matter how long it took and no matter how much studying and learning it would require, this seed could grow and reward him greatly, so he made it his purpose in life, stayed focused and reaped the reward.

If I know people, the way I think I know people, most would have looked at that mountain and the hard work required in extracting the gold, and they would have accepted the easy money offer. The danger of growing weary and giving up on doing what is right is that you don't reap the reward, but those who stay the course and don't give up will always reap the reward.

As I close this chapter, I hope that by now, you have a clearer understanding that knowing your purpose is exciting. It shows you that better is ahead. It brings you to an expected end. This is what God was telling the prophet, Jeremiah, "For I know the thoughts that I think toward you, saith the Lord, thoughts of peace, and not of evil, to give you an expected end" (Jeremiah 29:11 KJV). Purpose takes you to the expected end that God had assigned to your life from before the world began. He assigned it without your consultation and placed it in you without your knowledge. It was always God's divine plan for you to experience better, so to experience the fulfilment of your dreams in the future, stay focused on fulfilling your potential now.

"When you powerfully push to reach your potential,
your life's purpose will have no choice but to manifest to the world."

SHAWN BREMNER

3

The Blessing in Believing

He replied, "Because you have so little faith.
Truly I tell you, if you have faith as small as a
mustard seed, you can say to this mountain,
'Move from here to there,' and it will move.
Nothing will be impossible for you."

(Matt. 17:20 NIV)

Faith is one of the most talked-about subjects in the entire Bible. More than 388 times, the word faith is mentioned. Hebrews 11:6 tells us why it's so important; it says, "And without faith, it is impossible to please God..." it is impossible because we first come into a relationship with God through this medium. Though we are saved by grace, it is through faith. Pleasing God occurs when we have faith and apply it.

How can we apply it? The writer of Hebrews gives us a description of what faith is and how it is to be used, "Now faith is the substance of things hope for, the evidence of things not seen"

(Heb. 11:1 KJV). His description describes it as having substance, though it cannot yet be seen. It is concrete, though it cannot yet be seen. The very thing it hopes for requires a leap of faith.

I've heard many people say they have faith, but they appear to be stationary; there is no movement, there is no motion, neither is there any activity. The faith discussed in the Bible has works attached to it, Faith without works is dead (James 2:26). Faith is the very thing that moves us towards the things we hope for, so it keeps us moving forward; even if the movement is slow and uneventful at first, we still keep moving. This is the kind of faith that is pleasing to God. I decided long ago that I want to be a God pleaser. "Walking by faith and not by sight" produces results; it won't be long before you see its fruit both present and eternal.

> *"To have faith is to have wings."*
>
> JAMES M BARRIE

Some of the older generations have disagreed with some modern technology and things such as online dating. They have even preached it from the pulpit as being wrong. They believe that you're just supposed to pray and then wait for God to bring that particular person into your life. I am not saying that you can't find your wife or husband that way, but the Bible does say, "He who finds a wife finds a good thing, and obtains favour from the Lord" (Prov. 18:22). Surely that is permission to go looking? You rarely find, without looking. One can have the faith to believe that you're going to find your significant other, but then you need "works" to be added to your faith, and if online dating is considered to be the "works," then why not. I have met many who have found love online and are very happy and, at the same token, met some who have found love the conventional way, who have been very unhappy. My point is faith needs works to produce the thing hoped for.

What or who drives you?

This being said, faith must move us. It becomes a driving force. It guides you, controls you and directs you. If it is not pushing and driving you forward, then we have to ask what is? Everyone's life is driven by something. By definition, the verb "drive" means to guide, to control and to direct. For example., when you are driving a car, at that precise moment, you are guiding, controlling and directing it. If you are driving a nail into a piece of wood, once again, at that very moment, you are guiding, controlling and directing it.

For the Christian, this is what our faith is supposed to do for us; it is supposed to drive us. We are supposed to operate, think and behave differently from those in the world. "Though we are in the world, we are not of the world," therefore, we have a different modus operandi.

It is not unusual for those of the world to allow problems to guide them or pressures to drive them, but we are told to cast all of our cares and worries upon the Lord, for He cares for us (1Peter 5:7). There are those in this world who even allow fear to be the driving factor in their lives. If fear and anxiety become your driving factor, it will cause you to miss out on so many opportunities and things that should rightfully be yours because it will convince you to always play it safe instead of venturing out with faith. Fear has torment; it can be a self-imposed prison that keeps you contained and stagnant.

I have also met some who allowed guilt to be the driving force in their life. The shame from past memories is manipulating and pushing them to try to correct a past that can no longer be corrected. The wonderful thing about being in Christ is that your past no longer matters; Christ has taken care of it so that you can now concentrate on your future. "If any man is in Christ, he is a new creature: old things are passed away; behold, all things have become new" (2 Cor. 5:17 KJV). We serve a God of more than a second chance; he offers yet another chance along with a fresh start. Faith then must be our driving force. God wants us to be visionaries. He wants us to dream and then use our faith to bring those things into our world.

We are made in the image and likeness of God, and God himself is the perfect example of a dreamer and visionary. The creation story in Genesis reveals how God looked at a mass of chaos that was existing without form and void and visualised something else; He saw what it could be and went to work. He took action and began to speak what he wanted to see, then transformed it into perfection.

"We may be products of our past, but we don't have to be imprisoned by it."

When God saw what He created, he said it was good. Imagine for a moment if God was not driven. Imagine if He was passive about His dream? Or if when God saw that formless substance, He sat around thinking, "This is long." What if he decided to just leave it and see what it would become on its own? Our world would not exist today. God is our perfect example. Look at the innate drive and desires that exist in God, our creator.

The fuel of passion

We were created in God's image and his likeness. We, too, were designed to dream. Dreams and visions are much more than just thoughts. A real dream is a concept with a passion. If there is no passion behind it, it ceases to be a real dream; it becomes no more than a thought. When passion infuses a dream, it will cause that person to stop at nothing until they achieve what is in their heart. They will pursue with purpose; they will use whatever resource available to create the possibility. God created humanity using dust from the earth; it doesn't come more creative than that. The perfect example has already been set.

I am a visionary by nature; I love to dream. I dream of a better life for my family. I dream of a better world for my children. I dream of better things for my church. Some of the things I dream about may seem farfetched to others, but I am just crazy enough to believe that with my faith in God "All things are possible to them that believe."

Martin Luther King Jr. was a dreamer too. On August 28, 1963, a year before I was born, in his Lincoln Memorial speech, he said, "I have a dream that one day this nation will rise up and live out the true meaning of its creed: we hold these truths to be self-evident; that all men are created equal. I have a dream that little children will one day live in a nation where they will not be judged by the colour of their skin but by the content of their character. I have a dream that one day every valley shall be exalted, every hill and mountain shall be made low, the rough places plain, and the crooked places will be made straight, and before the Lord will be revealed, and all flesh shall see it together. This is our hope. This is the faith that I go back to the mount with."

Dreaming of better is normal. We are supposed to dream, and although I am very much a dreamer and a believer, I will be the first to admit that sometimes, I find myself fighting a war in my mind. Always remaining positive and only saying the things that encourage faith is a challenge. Make no mistake about it, things will always come to challenge your faith and try to push you into doubt. It reminds me of that desperate father in Mark 9:24 who had a demon-possessed son, which he brought to Jesus' disciples. He pleaded with them to help his son, but they could not help. So, when he saw Jesus come down from the mountain, he ran and cried out to Jesus, "If you can do anything, have mercy on us and help us." Jesus replied in such a lovely way, "All things are possible to them that believe." The father cried out, "I do believe; help me overcome my unbelief!"

This man had faith to believe, but there was a war going on in his mind. The enemy is always trying to get us to doubt in our minds; however, when this doubt tries to come, don't entertain it. Remain committed and convicted. Keep walking by faith, which means we are in motion, moving all the time towards that thing hoped for, and you will receive it by faith.

"Faith is taking the first step, even when you don't see the whole staircase."

DR MARTIN LUTHER KING JR.

The peril of doubting

I have spoken quite a bit about what faith is and what faith does, but now I want to show you what faith is not. Faith is never disbelief. A person's faith may waver from time to time, but when faith gets to the point where it disbelieves, it is no longer faith but disbelief. This is where the enemy wants you. He wants you so far gone the other way that you believe his lies and disbelieve God's truth.

Though Jesus never called him "Doubting Thomas," he inherited this name because of his honest statement of disbelief. Thomas said, "Unless I see the nail marks in his hands and put my finger where the nails were, and put my hand into his side, I will not believe" (John 20:25 NKJV).

Here is a man who wanted verifiable proof before he would dare to believe. Some of us have no right to ever refer to him as - Doubting Thomas unless we are willing to put "doubting" before our name too. It reminds me of what my mother would say in such situations; she would say, "Isn't this the pot calling the kettle black?"

> *"I believe though I do not comprehend, and I hold by faith what I cannot grasp with the mind."*
>
> SAINT BERNARD OF CLAIRVAUX

Thomas simply didn't believe; does that sound familiar? Have you ever been sick and not really thought that God was going to heal you? Or, have you ever been in need and not believed Paul's declaration that God shall supply all your needs according to His riches in glory? In fact, Thomas' situation goes deeper than that; he refused to believe. That is how subtle disbelief can be, but when you get to the stage where you give up hope altogether, that is when you are no longer in faith, you have crossed the line into disbelief. Except for the mercies of God, don't ever expect to receive a blessing that way. "For let not that man think that he shall receive anything of the Lord" (James 1:7 KJV).

Thomas doesn't believe but he verbalises it. It does not just remain a thought in his head. No! he puts wings on it and allows it to fly out of his mouth, and although Jesus was not there to hear it, He knew exactly what was said. Jesus hears every faithless word we speak. But what I love about grace is that it freely affords us the very thing we don't deserve. Thomas' disbelief should disqualify him totally from the blessing of seeing the resurrected Saviour, but Jesus blesses him with His presence regardless.

When Jesus walks into the room and appears before the disciples for the second time - Thomas, now being present, Jesus turns to him and says, "Thomas put your finger here, and look at my hands. Put your hand into the wound in my side. Don't be faithless any longer. Believe!"

Immediately after speaking, Thomas cries out, "My Lord and my God." Jesus then replies, "Thomas, you believe because you have seen me. Blessed are those who believe without seeing me." Right there, Jesus was referring to you and me, and all those who would come to him later, those who would live in a different time and space. Jesus was saying; there is a blessing coming to all those who believe in Him even though they never witnessed His life; those who believe, though they never witnessed His crucifixion and his death; those who never witnessed His resurrection and ascension yet still choose to believe.

It confirms just how important it is to believe, even though you haven't yet seen, and this is regarding our faith in him and our faith in what he wants to do in our lives. The blessings of Christ are ours simply because we believe.

With this said, do you believe that God wants you to be successful in all areas of life? It is what the apostle John was speaking about when he wrote, "Beloved; I pray that you may prosper in all things and be in health, just as your soul prospers" (3 John1:2 YLT). This kind of prosperity refers to every area of our lives, but doubt and disbelief will rob you of it. Doubting that God wants to heal you will rob you of your health. Doubting that God wants to supply all your needs according to His riches in glory will keep you suffocating in need. There is great peril in doubt but a great blessing in believing. We are called believers for a reason, so let's live up to that name in all aspects. If these blessings are what God wills for us, let's grab them with both hands by faith.

Faith of any kind has always come by hearing. A person doesn't believe they are dumb until they hear somebody tell them they're stupid. I have met many who have erroneously believed this lie after hearing it many times. Others didn't see themselves as unattractive until they heard somebody say they were ugly. You didn't think you were incapable of learning until you heard somebody tell you that you could never learn anything. These are all lies the enemy feed us, but anything you hear enough builds your belief. Faith and believing come by hearing. What is it you believe about yourself?

Not only are we to believe in God, but we are to believe in ourselves too. Notice how apostle Paul puts it in Phil. 4:13, he says, "I can do all things through Christ who strengthens me." Before he brings up Christ, he brings up himself. "I can." He truly believes that he can do all things with Christ. What would happen if you really believed that? How differently would you act if you really believed that? I think you would walk around with your head held high with a straight back. Nobody would be able to intimidate you at any time, in any place. Can you imagine how confident you would appear if you walked into your next job interview and they asked you what can you do, and you replied, "I can do all things?" They would be amazed by your confidence. It is the confidence God wants us to have in Him.

Many of us quote this scripture but do we really believe it? Whoever you are reading this book, I'm pleading with you, don't only recite this verse but believe it with all your heart. God has given every man a measure of faith because it would be wrong for salvation to be based on belief and God not give you enough belief to be saved, and the same way you used your faith to receive salvation, use it to believe that things are getting better in your life. There is a blessing in believing.

"Credo ut intelligam."
I believe in order to understand.

ST ANSELM OF CANTERBURY

4

Fear – Friend or Foe

*Then I said to you, "Do not be terrified; do not be
afraid of them. The LORD your God, who is going
before you, will fight for you, as he did for you in
Egypt, before your very eyes, and in the wilderness.
There you saw how the LORD your God carried
you, as a father carries his son, all the way you
went until you reached this place." In spite of this,
you did not trust in the LORD your God.*

(Deut.1:29-32 KJV)

The first inauguration of Franklin D. Roosevelt as the 32nd
President of the United States was held on Saturday, March 4, 1933,
at the East Portico of the United States Capitol in Washington, D.C.
This 37th inauguration marked the commencement of the first
term of Franklin D. Roosevelt as President and John Nance Garner
as Vice President. In his 20-minute-long inaugural address,
consisting of 1,883 words, President Roosevelt uttered some
words that will forever be remembered. He said, "The only thing

we have to fear is fear itself." Since that day, these words have been repeated time and time again. It might surprise you to know that God spoke to us about fear thousands of years earlier. God has always spoken to us about fear; in fact, the phrase "Do not be afraid" is presented to us in scripture 365 times. Littered throughout the pages of the Bible, more than the command to love, pray and forgive is that command "Do not be afraid."

Throughout the Bible, every time God called somebody to do something significant, fear was their response. When God calls Gideon, Gideon was hiding in a winepress, and God had to tell him, "Do not be afraid, When God called Jeremiah, his response was "I'm just a boy", and when Jeremiah got through talking, God had to tell him "Do not be afraid." Isaiah was known as the eagle-eyed prophet, and even he had to be told the same. The list goes on; the scriptures are replete with people who were confronted with fear.

The reason the command "Do not fear" is so prevalent in the Bible is because fear is commonplace in life. Isn't it ironic that 365 times we are commanded not to fear, and that is the number of days we have in any one year? If you are going to walk into the better life and success that God has called you to, if you're going to do exploits, if you are going to pursue the abundant life that God is calling you to do, you cannot allow fear to dictate.

Why is fear so displeasing to God?

No one is immune to fear. It doesn't matter how big and strong you are. It doesn't matter how many degrees you have on your wall, how much money you make, what position you hold in society; all of us have moments when we are challenged by fear. Still, even though fear may be common, fear is not God's will for the believer; it never has been and never will be. God doesn't want his children ever to be controlled by fear. Fear has torment, brings anxiety, produces worry and results in stress.

The scripture tells us that fear doesn't come from God, "God has not given us a spirit of fear, but of power and of love and of a sound mind" (1Tim1:7). John tells us, "There is no fear in love; but perfect love casteth out fear: because fear hath torment. He that feareth is not made perfect in love."

It is important to note that there are at least two types of fear spoken about in the Bible, so it is necessary to make the distinction. Firstly, the Hebrew word yārē' seen in the Old Testament, speaks of having a fear of a thing happening. It is to look at something that is coming your way and fear its effect, that is to be in a state of feeling great distress and deep concern of pain or unfavourable circumstance. It refers commonly to experiencing an emotional reaction.

Secondly, there is the Hebrew word paḥad. This fear is rooted in reverence. It speaks of identifying that something has power, and you're terrified by what it could do because of the power it holds. It is having awe or reverence towards a thing or person. It is the only type of fear we should have. This reverential fear should be towards our God. We often hear this fear with the phrase "The fear of the Lord."

Sometimes fear in the Bible is yārē, and other times it is paḥad when we read the Bible, we have to make the distinction. Paḥad is used when you are speaking about the sovereignty of God; you ought to have a healthy fear and reverence for the authority of God. When you think of the eternal, omnipotent God, there ought to be awe and utmost respect.

So, from this, we can see there is a spirit of fear, yārē and there is also the fear of the Lord paḥad. A spirit of fear is unhealthy. It is consuming and paralyzing but the fear of the Lord is healthy and necessary. A spirit of fear is foolish while fearing God is the beginning of wisdom. A spirit of fear debilitates; the fear of the Lord empowers. When a spirit of fear brings death, the fear of the Lord offers life.

The New Testament, however, introduces yet another word for fear phobeō. The range of meaning for phobeō covers the full spectrum of expected contexts, such as fearing physical danger, fearing social ramifications, feeling awe at witnessing extraordinary events, fearing the wrath of God, or feeling reverence and respect for God.

> "What makes us so afraid is the thing we half see, or half hear, as in a wood at dusk, when a tree stump becomes an animal and a sound becomes a siren. And most of that fear is the fear of not knowing, of not actually seeing correctly."
>
> EDNA O' BRIEN

Jesus said, in Luke 12:4-5, "Do not be afraid of those who kill the body, and after that have no more that they can do. But I will show you whom you should fear: Fear Him who, after He has killed, has the power to cast into hell; yes, I say to you, fear Him!" That is the kind of fear that phobeō sometimes refers to and paḥad always refers to. As children of God, we are to fear the Lord but have no fear for anything or anyone else because as you now see, when you fear something, you can be reverencing it. When you fear it, it is like you are kneeling before it. When you fear a thing, you are ascribing it power over your life, which is why fear is so displeasing to the Lord.

Many people do not experience better in life because they allow fear yārē to paralyse them. It keeps them from moving into what is rightfully theirs. We see this with the Children of Israel when they sent spies into the Promised Land to check it out. The spies came back with a negative report. It was negative because of the attitude in which they perceived it and the way they relayed it. They said, ...We went to the land where you sent us. It truly flows with milk and honey, and this is its fruit. Nevertheless, the people who dwell in the land are strong; we are not able to go up against the people, for they are stronger than we are and we were like grasshoppers in our own sight, and so we were in their sight (Number 13:27-32).

Who told them that they were being perceived as grasshoppers? Why is our perception of ourselves so wrong? If we could only see ourselves the way God sees us! God has already told us that we are "the head and not the tail, that we are above and not beneath." If only they had seen themselves correctly, perhaps they would have responded differently. It was this, along with fear, that made a three-week journey become that forty-year struggle.

Most of that generation never walked into the Promised Land that God said was theirs. In Deuteronomy, chapter one, Moses speaks to the next generation of Israelites and tells them exactly why the previous generation missed out. Sadly, it was fear.

There is a danger in fear. When you fear, you run the risk of reverencing and ascribing the authority to something or someone that only God should be receiving from you. Why would you give anything or anyone else that kind of elevated place in your life?

The negative attraction of fear

Please understand that fear works like faith. Just as faith always activates God, fear always activates Satan. Whilst you're operating in faith, you can be positive that God will come through for you in every situation, but when you begin to let fear and mistrust be a part of your thought pattern, you give the enemy the foothold he needs.

Fear has pulling power. Firstly, it predicts the worst, envisions the worst-case scenario, convinces you of a gloomy future, and attracts a negative outcome. That is the power it has. It was Job who said, "The very thing I fear has come upon me" (Job 3:25 KJV). It is interesting that a man like Job, who was righteous and upright, a man who stayed away from evil, could fear something happening, and that very thing he feared became a reality.

Another story that is worth lending our attention to is found in 1 Kings 18 - 19. It clearly displays the danger of giving in to the yārē kind of fear. Ahab, who had become Israel's king, chose to marry an evil woman called Jezebel. She had an evil influence on him.

Together they led Israel to abandon the worshipping of the true God Jehovah for the worship of pagan gods.

Queen Jezebel silenced anyone who dared to worship Jehovah publicly; she even tried to find prophets of God to kill them. Elijah, God's prophet, warned Ahab to repent and return Israel to their God, but because he refused, Israel had experienced over three years of famine and drought.

At the end of the three years, Elijah confronted King Ahab again, and he fearlessly challenged the prophets of Baal in one of the most famous showdowns in the Bible. With a tremendous display of power, God showed up for Elijah, then, in another act of extreme courage, Elijah executed all those wicked prophets of Baal. He prayed to God, and the three-year drought came to a miraculous end.

"Fear is simply faith in what Satan says."

Z NTLANGULA

However, not long after this victory, despite all that courage and fearless obedience he showed to God, Elijah received a threatening message from Queen Jezebel that terrified him. It stated, by this time tomorrow, she would do to Elijah what he had done to the prophets of Baal. She vowed to kill him. Despite everything God had done in the previous twenty-four hours to prove Himself, all Elijah could think of was all the prophets Jezebel had already killed. It was clear what type of fear engulfed him, 'yārē'. It caused him to run for his life until he was exhausted. One threat from this evil woman caused him to be defeated in mind and body, and the Bible says he laid down under a tree and begged God to end his life.

As stated previously, this kind of fear is devastatingly crippling; it robs us of the glorious success that God has for each one of us. In his tender mercies, God visited Elijah in his time of need and miraculously ministered to his physical needs, providing food, water and giving him a much-needed rest to prepare for a forty-day and night journey into the wilderness. Elijah was then led to Mount Sinai; this was a significant place; it was the famous mountain, where God previously showed Himself to Moses and the children of Israel on many occasions.

After resting there, God spoke to Elijah and addressed his fear. It is interesting how God chooses to talk to Elijah this time. God didn't show up in a terrible windstorm, or a mighty earthquake, or the blazing fire. But God showed up in a still small voice and gave Elijah instructions on how to go forward. Although Jezebel's issued threat instilled fear, all Elijah needed was a word from God in a still small voice. One word spoken from God amid fear can make all the difference. The root of Elijah's fear was not a lack of faith in God's power (he always knew God was all-powerful), but it was a lack of trust in His plan. He didn't understand the plan of God, and so when he heard the small threatening voice of an evil woman, he doubted the plan of God.

God has a plan for all of us; it is a plan to prosper us. He tells us this in Psalms 33:11, "The plans of the LORD stand firm forever, the purposes of His heart through all generations." God has an "already planned success" with your name on it. Don't ever allow the pulling power of fear to kill, steal and destroy what is rightfully yours. I come with a still small voice to tell you that God is with you. He always has been, and he promises to go ahead of you. He is already in that surgery before you even go in; he is already in that conversation that you are afraid to have. He is already in that exam before you even sit down at the desk because he goes ahead of you. This is what Moses told the children of Israel in Deut. 1:30 The LORD your God, who is going before you, will fight for you, as he did for you in Egypt". God goes before us, and He has a plan to bring you to an expected end, so don't fear.

Right now, we are living in unprecedented times. It is the first time my generation has had to endure a pandemic. Up until now, we had only heard about such things and the devastation they can cause. Fear has gripped our nation like never before. People are afraid to walk the streets, go shopping, attend school, and some are even afraid to go into certain parts of their own homes if others are currently there. Our government hasn't helped the situation either. Every day they tell us of more deaths from up and down the country. One could ask, isn't it normal to fear in such times, given the circumstances? No! Being concerned and being fearful are two different things. Fear has torment, and it works much like faith in that it pulls things our way but with a negative effect.

When we fear, we no longer believe God is in control. When we remember the phrase "fear not" is in the Bible 365 times, it should cause us to understand that the devil sends things to elicit fear every day. If we were to succumb to fear every day, we would be a nervous wreck; we would never venture anywhere. Fear is a highly damaging emotion that cripples you, but it is also described as a spirit that we must reject. Remember, "God has not given us a spirit of fear" (1 Tim 1: 7 KJV). Even in a pandemic such as this, we must believe "Better" is ahead. Fear will try to get you to believe the worst and pull the worst towards you, so we must resist it and continue to believe in "Better."

"Never let fear decide your future."

5

Knowing the Enemy of Better

But they did not prevail, nor was a place found
for them in heaven any longer. So, the great
dragon was cast out, that serpent of old, called
the Devil and Satan, who deceives the whole
world; he was cast to the earth, and his angels
were cast out with him.

(Rev. 12:8-9 NKJV)

In whatever field of battle, you are in; it is important that you seek to know your enemy; your success over him depends on it. What tactics does he deploy? What thought process does he engage? What is his greatest weakness? What are his strengths? If you want to gain an advantage over your enemy, it's imperative that you study him. Our adversary has no power or authority over you except that which you allow. He is an imposter pretending to be a big bad lion. Peter says, "Our adversary the devil walks around like a roaring lion" This word 'like' speaks of "possessing the characteristics of, resembling closely". It means he appears to be something he is not; good at acting and sounding like a lion, but he is not a lion. He has been a liar and a deceiver from the beginning. This is his "modus operandi," so Peter admonishes us to be sober and vigilant (1Pet. 5:8 KJV). The devil prowls around looking for someone to devour." The devil knows he cannot take away our salvation because the Holy Ghost has sealed that, but he will try to destroy our faith and trust in God. If he can shake our trust in God, he is halfway there to destroying our dream of "Better."

The more you know about him, the better your strategy can be in overcoming him. Satan is the chief enemy of the believer. Trust me when I tell you, he has studied you and he has been studying you a long time. He knows what makes you weak and tailors his temptations to fit your nature. If it made your father fail, he will try it on you; if it made your mother slip, he will send it your way. He has studied you and your family. He has monitored your bloodline and, with what he has seen in your bloodline, uses it in whatever way he can. He knows what you have a penchant for, he knows what you have a propensity to do, and he seeks to tie you down in those generational curses that have long existed in your family line. This is where it becomes really personal. Like a violent animal studying its prey, he lurks behind bushes, camouflaging himself, waiting for the best moment to pounce in order to destroy before better can find you.

Generational curses

The one thing the devil uses that is not talked about nearly enough, is generational curses. A Generational Curse is a reoccurring problem that seeks to move from generation to generation. None of us can choose our relatives any more than we can choose our race, gender or skin colour. Yet somebody up the family tree can give a spirit the right to visit the family because of a sin or iniquity they commit.

Curses cannot visit a family without a cause. The Bible states that "the iniquity of the father can be visited upon the children unto the third and fourth generation" (Exo. 20:5 KJV). Sometimes you can be struggling with something and not realise that you are fighting your grandfather's or great grandmother's demon, and although this may appear to be unfair, it is a reality. Generational curses are real, and they manifest themselves in a myriad of ways. Listed below are just some examples of how and where generational curses can show up.

> *"If you didn't come from a healthy family, you can make sure a healthy family comes from you."*
>
> JESSICA OLIVER

The curse of family sickness

Sicknesses can be the result of a generational curse. When you read Deuteronomy 28:21, it speaks about a person being smitten with diseases such as "consumption, fever, inflammation, extreme burning, sword and blasting and with mildew" and that these things can pursue you until you perish and die. These kinds of curses release many types of sicknesses. For example, consumption can manifest itself as a wasting lung disease, emphysema, and lung cancer. "Inflammation" is mentioned too, indicating sicknesses that are evidenced by arthritis etc. Inflammation can cause many illnesses, and when in the brain, it can lead to Alzheimer. We also read the term "extreme burning." This point toward all sorts of strange fevers.

Menstrual problems, bareness and impotence, can be the result of a family curse also. Scripture says, in Deut. 28:18 "Cursed shall be the fruit of thy body, and the fruit of thy land, the increase of thy kine, and the flocks of thy sheep." I would often hear women speak of menstrual problems as "The curse." The body mentioned in this text refers to the womb and abdomen, "Beten" is the Hebrew word used. It speaks of the reproduction system, including infections, hormone problems, menstrual problems, PMS, cramps, fibroids, barrenness, miscarriages, cysts, tumours, bladder problems, and much more. Men, too, can manifest this kind of curse with things like erectile dysfunction and impotence.

The curse of aimlessness

*And thou shalt grope at noonday as the blind
gropes in darkness, and thou shalt not prosper in
thy ways: and thou shalt be only oppressed and
spoiled evermore, and no man shall save thee.*

(Deut.28: 29 KJV)

Do you know that a simple thing like wandering through life and not having a vision for being better or a goal for your life can be indicative of a curse? People who live this way, hostile, with no ambition and without any thought or care of tomorrow, are who the Bible describes as blind men with no direction. They grope in the dark full of apathy, and they are lukewarm. When this kind of attitude is seen in a family individual, watch it carefully, because we were all created to be and do so much more than this. We are supposed to live with purpose, and purpose will lead us to a better life.

Relational curses

Thy sons and thy daughters shall be given
unto another people, and thine eyes shall look,
and fail with longing for them all the day long:
and there shall be no might in thine hand.

(Deut.28:32)

Divorce and family breakdown can also be a manifestation of a generational curse. This causes families to be estranged and children to be scattered. There was a time in our country where 50% of first marriages ended in divorce and 67% of second marriages followed suit, and of course, this brought a devastating effect on the children. Now sadly, we are told this number has increased, and things have gotten worse.

This excellent institution called marriage that God beautifully designed to increase our happiness, bring fulfilment and be the proper way to bring children into our world is being attacked left, right and centre by the enemy. When the devil breaks up a home, it can have a devastating effect on the children. Remember, Satan comes to steal, kill and destroy. He is not only trying to destroy you and your future success; he is also trying to destroy whatever better life is destined for our children and the next generation, and he knows just how to do it; he has a plan.

Financial curses

Cursed shall be thy basket and thy store.

(Deut. 28:17 KJV)

A financial curse will keep you in lack and poverty. A person under this curse will squander, waste and get further in debt and bondage and most times will not be able to see their way clear. A financial curse is operating to kill your financial success, but there is hope in God. Listen to what the Bible says, "God is able to make all grace abound toward you; that ye, always having all sufficiency in all things, may abound to every good work" (2 Cor. 9: 8 KJV).

Though I have mentioned just a few generational curses seen from Scripture, there are many others. Curses do not come upon individuals without a cause. For it to be a generational curse, someone up the family tree got involved in some sin or iniquity that caused that curse to filter down. They were the originator, but you can be the finisher. You can decide, "This curse goes no further down this bloodline; the buck stops with me."

> *It's up to us to break generational curses, when they say, "it runs in the family" you tell them "this is where it runs out."*
>
> THE MINDS JOURNAL

Once a curse is identified, it can be broken; there is deliverance through the blood of Jesus. These curses can and must be broken. When they are broken, you are set free, and your children and grandchildren are freed too. Break it in Jesus' name, for the Bible says whom the Son sets free is free indeed (John 8:36 KJV).

Three-pronged attack

Another thing Scriptures tell us about our enemy is that he has a three-fold desire. He wants to steal, kill and destroy; that is his agenda. In his arsenal, he uses weapons we've seen before in scripture; we see them as early as in Genesis in the Garden of Eden; the lust of the flesh, the lust of the eyes, and the pride of life (1 John 2:15-16 KJV). I want to show you that the devil uses the same tools today, only reconfigured and tweaked for this generation.

What used to be considered wrong has now been accepted as right. As long as it feels good, you're encouraged to do it. Wrong is promoted on our TV screens. It's seen on street posters. It taught in our schools as being an alternative way. Whatever perversion you are interested in can now come to you by way of your computer screen, with a click of a button. All of this is fulfilling that which the flesh is lusting for and what the eye longs to see.

Cyberspace has become the "Go to" place for satisfaction. There is a website for everything; there is a chat room of choice for you to join without even disclosing who you are; nobody has to know your name. When I first learnt to drive, I remember getting lost one day in a particular area of London. I ended up going down an unknown street and, to my horror, saw ladies of the night standing on the street corners. Men would pull their cars up to the pavement to solicit them, but now people no longer have to go out to fulfil that desire; they can now order an escort online without ever leaving their homes. He still desires to trap you; he still wants to ensnare you; he has just found a different way to do it. Remember, the Bible states that "Satan is a liar." When he lies, he speaks what is natural to him, for he is a liar and the father of lies and half-truths (John 8:44 AMP).

Paul reminds us in 2 Cor. 2:11 that, "We are not ignorant of his devices." Of course not, because we have seen them before. He doesn't have anything new up his sleeves, but yet so many of us still become victims even when we know his objective and his weapons? How is it that we are still tricked and deceived by him time and time again? Remember, I told you the devil studies you, and he examines you close up; he is closer to you than you realise because he resides here on earth. He was cast out of heaven, and he is here to deceive the whole world.

Therefore rejoice, you heavens and you who dwell in them! But woe to the earth and the sea, because the devil has gone down to you! He is filled with fury, because he knows that his time is short.

(Rev. 12:12 KJV)

Heaven is happy that Satan has gone because there is no longer war in heaven but woe to the earth's inhabitants and the seas now that Satan is here. The Bible says, "The devil has come with great wrath, and he is filled with fury."

He wants to destroy everything he can, not only on earth but everything in the waters too. This means, not only do we as humans have to watch out, but all the animals, all the creatures of the earth and all the inhabitants of the sea need to also keep watch too. That is why everything is such a mess. The animals on earth, the fish in our seas and humanity on our streets are all out of control.

We see animals turning on each other, humans fighting each other, household pets out of control and mauling humans on the street! It wasn't too long ago they reported a fox accessing someone's house through the back door and attacking a baby lying in his cot. Things changed the moment Satan was cast out of heaven.

Shortened time

And except those days should be shortened,
there should no flesh be saved: but for the
elect's sake those days shall be shortened.

(Matt. 24:22 KJV)

The enemy is angry, and his time is short, so he has to be strategic if he wants to be effective. For over seven thousand years, the Devil has been at work, deceiving people with the aim of stealing from them, killing and destroying them. He has mastered his craft; if he doesn't get you the first time, he may leave you for a season but returns just like he did when tempting Jesus in the wilderness (Matthew 4:11 KJV).

He is persistent and determined, don't give him an inch, or he will take a yard. He always seeks to take more than you allow him to. Once you permit him an area in which to roam, he will break down barriers and won't stop until he takes more territory.

Why we must win

The Bible tells us the wages of sin is death (Rom. 6:23 KJV). What the devil wants to do more than anything else is bring death. It is not just physical or spiritual death but death to your success, dreams, visions, and aspirations. Have you had a dream that you didn't pursue? Or perhaps an aspiration that died over time? Who killed that dream? Somebody recently told me the reason she didn't pursue more of her dreams; she said it was because of a family member. This may appear to be the reason, but even if a family member dissuaded you, it was the devil who was ultimately behind its death.

I want to encourage you to resurrect it. You were born to be successful; you were born to be fruitful and multiply, it's in your DNA, but sin is a destroyer. James 1:15 says, "Then when lust hath conceived, it brings forth sin: and sin when it is finished, brings forth death." Sin may feel good in the moment but goes to work behind the scenes, destroying what could have been and ruining what should have been; that's why we are told to resist the devil, along with his temptations, resist him, and he will flee (James 4:7).

My brothers and sisters, I urge you, whoever you are and wherever you are reading this book, make a commitment right now to never again knowingly and consciously give in to the devil's temptation to do what you know displeases God. If you know it is a wrong act, then you'll also know the devil sent it. He is the enemy of better.

It took me a while to realise that all the devil can do is suggest things. He cannot force you to do anything. He suggests and plants thoughts as seeds in your head. He uses the power of suggestion. Have you ever watched a food advertisement on TV and suddenly felt hungry? Or perhaps watched somebody yawn and felt a compulsion to do the same? The more you see something or think about something, the stronger its pull is. We tend to move towards what we are focussing on. That is why most diets don't work because they keep you thinking about food and what you can eat, which only makes you hungrier.

Whatever captures your attention, arouses your emotions, and in turn, your emotions activate your behaviour. It is why we must change our focus and control our thoughts. The devil wants to get you dirty and stained with sin again, but we have been given authority "to cast down imaginations, and every high thing that exalts itself against the knowledge of God, and to bring into captivity every thought to the obedience of Christ" (2 Cor. 10:5).

I recently heard a story of a little boy who played in the woods just a short distance away from the dilapidated hut he lived in. His parents were too poor to buy him any toys, so he had to make do with whatever he could find. One day he chanced upon a stone that was unlike any that he had ever seen. The polished surface of the stone glistened in his hands and winked at him each time he turned it around in the sunlight. It was his very own treasure, and he loved it. The boy did not dare bring it back to his home because there was nowhere in the hut where he could hide it. He decided to dig a deep hole under some bushes and hide his precious possession there.

The next day the boy couldn't' wait to retrieve his stone and ran to its hiding place as soon as the sun arose. When his fingers finally found the stone in its muddy hideaway, it was grubby and stained, without the lustre that he loved so much. The boy took the stone to the stream and carefully dipped it in, allowing the dirt to be washed away. Finally, it was clean again, and the boy's heart swelled with pride at his converted find. But all too soon, the time came for the boy to head home, and he had to return the stone to its hiding place.

Every day the boy would rush to the spot where he had hidden the stone. And every day, he would find its shiny surface smeared with mud, and he would walk to the river some distance away to wash it. After having to do this for many days, he decided to solve the problem. That day when it was almost time for him to head home, the little boy took his stone to a small waterfall and wedged it carefully under a rock, right in the middle of the steady flow of the waterfall. That night the stone experienced a continual washing and the little boy never had to wash the stone again. Every time he retrieved it, it gleamed in his hands, thoroughly cleansed.

This is how God wants us to position ourselves, right under the rock and in the middle of the steady flow where we can remain cleansed. The songwriter William Cowper put it this way, "There is a fountain filled with blood, drawn from Immanuel's veins, and sinners plunged beneath that flood lose all their guilty stains."

God doesn't want us to be smeared and dirty with sin every day but to resist evil and stay washed and sanctified. Paul said, "...Just as Christ loved the church and gave Himself up for her to sanctify her, cleansing her by the washing with water through the word, and to present her to Himself as a glorious church, without stain or wrinkle or any such blemish, but holy and blameless" (Eph. 5:25-27).

Christ gave himself so that we could be cleansed once and for all and that is how he wants us to remain. So, let's be committed to this process of remaining cleansed. There is a difference between making a decision and making a commitment. Although they sound similar, decisions can be made easily because decisions are made with the brain. Commitments, on the other hand, are different; they are made with your heart. Commitments are longer lasting and harder to break. They go much further; they are transformational. Commitments bring results and birth success, so let's commit to the process of doing better so we can experience better.

Next, we will examine some of the obstacles that position themselves in the way of our progress to obtaining a better life. It may surprise you to learn how often such things are overlooked.

*"To forgive is to set a prisoner free
and discover that the prisoner was you."*

LEWIS B. SMEDES

6

Removing an Obstacle to Better

Take heed to yourselves. If your brother sins
against you, rebuke him; and if he repents, forgive
him. And if he sins against you seven times in a
day, and seven times in a day returns to you,
saying, 'I repent,' you shall forgive him." And the
apostles said to the Lord, "Increase our faith."

(Luke 17:3-5 NKJ)

One of the most hidden and yet successful obstacles to significant progress is unforgiveness. If I were to ask you if you've ever been hurt, and if so, when was the last time it happened? Perhaps some of you wouldn't have to think back too far. Still, I can guarantee there are some, who although, may have to go back several years, can admit that in some cases, the hurt was so deep they remember it like it was yesterday. They remember everything about the event, what day of the week it was, what they were wearing, and how it felt because some experiences hurt so bad that they leave an indelible mark on your heart. I bring this to your attention not to make you relive the experience but to make you aware that unforgiven and unforgotten incidences such as these can be obstacles standing in the way of you experiencing a better life. They strategically position themselves as landmines buried between you and your future.

I grew up hearing that time is a healer, but there are some wounds that are still as sensitive today as when they first happened. One such incident occurred when I was about thirteen years old. Back in those days, we didn't have much and "hand me downs" were a way of life. I remember having to wear my elder brother's trousers, which were far too big for me in length and width. To ensure it would stay up, my mother turned over the waistband about three times around my waist, and this also made it short enough to sit on my shoes. Then to ensure that nobody would see this temporary fix, she put a long jumper on me and made sure it was pulled down sufficiently to prevent anybody from seeing.

Later that night, we had family friends over, most of whom were much older than I was. While I was stood in the middle of the room, someone who knew what I was trying to hide underneath my jumper asked me to lift my hands, and the moment I did, he lifted my jumper to expose the fix that my mother had tried to cover up causing everybody to see and laugh.

Even at that early age, I wanted the ground to open and swallow me up. Now to others, this may have seemed liked such a small thing, but for me, that experience was crushing, especially being young and still trying to find myself. I remember it with such clarity. I didn't know if I would ever be able to like or forgive that individual again but thank God; time is a healer. There are all kinds of hurts that we will experience in this journey called life, and if we don't have some mechanism for dealing with them, they may continually hold us back from being who we are called to be and from achieving what we are supposed to achieve.

I believe this is what Jesus was doing with his disciples in Luke 17. He opens the chapter by telling them that it is impossible to be my disciple and not experience offences. Offences will come; in fact, it comes with the territory of being alive and having to mix with other individuals. Jesus hand-picked his disciples and knew that all of them would at some point experience an offence of some sort that could possibly derail them, and so to warn them, He tells them outright that "OFFENCES WILL COME."

The wounding effect of an offence is one of the most productive tools in the enemy's armoury. He uses it to not only ruin your relationships with others here on earth but also to destroy your relationship with God in heaven. What I'm trying to convey is that when you have been hurt and wounded, and when life has brought an offence your way, the devil seeks to inflict a psychological scar that is so bad that it holds you hostage to that pain. Anytime this happens, and you refuse to break free, you get stuck in that moment. How can God bless a person who is trapped in that kind of mess?

"Weak people revenge. Strong people forgive. intelligent people ignore."

ALBERT EINSTEIN

These followers of Jesus were about to be the church leaders, and Jesus was sending them out to establish ground and take territory in his kingdom. They were going to achieve a standard, a level and a height in ministry and leadership, and Jesus didn't want anything the enemy threw at them to be able to bring them down from where He was going to set them. It was as if Jesus was saying, 'it's essential that you have a system of managing negative things and negative people that come against you from the beginning.' So, with this, Jesus gives them the most valuable piece of advice for handling hurt; He says, "It doesn't matter what they throw at you, keep on forgiving them. As fast as they can throw it, throw it off. As fast as they send it, let it go." Jesus knew that one of the most effective weapons the devil uses from his armoury is offence. So, Jesus gave them the answer.

Forgiveness - the better option

The word 'forgiveness' has been defined in many ways, for example, to lay aside, to let alone, to send away, to clear the record and to forget. The call of God on our lives requires that we live a life of forgiveness, that we're able to take the things people do to us, the things people say about us, the hurts they inflict on us and forgive. It is what God requires of us daily, that as soon as we have been done wrong, to give it over straightaway. Please don't allow it to grow; don't let it to develop into bitterness. We are given a limited time to hold onto it; in fact, the Bible says, "Don't allow the sun to go down on your wrath" (Eph. 4:26). In other words, please don't allow the evening to come and find you still mulling over it in your mind. No, deal with it!

Most of us will confess that forgiving is not really on our agenda when we've been hurt really bad; when we've been cut deeply, forgiving is not instinctive. To forgive never feels like a natural response when people have done you wrong. Retaliation and revenge feel more natural; cussing them feels more satisfying, and getting your own back feels more rewarding. It's at those times, we like to remember the scriptures such as, "An eye for an eye and a tooth for a tooth." Do you remember that one? Exodus 21:24 because revenge feels natural, and yet we are told to forgive. Why? Because forgiving is one of the most beneficial and critical commands that God gives us to release us from pain. It also preserves intimacy in our relationship with God.

And as thy days, so shall thy strength be.

(Deut. 3:25 KJV)

There are health and safety authorities whose jobs are to warn us of things that are hazardous to our lives. They list things such as asbestos, corrosive and toxic materials, harmful liquids, and irritants on their websites. Whilst all of these are extremely dangerous and should be listed, there is yet another, but of course, one wouldn't expect it to be mentioned on such sites. However, it is my job to bring it to your attention; it's the danger associated with prolonged unforgiveness.

To refuse to forgive and to take your anger and hurt into the next day is hazardous to your health, to say the least. Therefore, we are commanded in Scripture to live one day at a time. We do not have enough strength to manage yesterday's pain today. Jesus said, "Sufficient unto the day is the evil thereof" (Matt 6:32). We could change that in the light of the above text to say 'Sufficient unto the day is the strength thereof,' because whatever evil the day serves up, God will give us the needed strength for that day, if we live day-by-day.

I'm convinced this is why so many suffer from illnesses such as hypertension, arthritis, diabetes, heart trouble, etc. People are ageing much too early due to carrying issues and offences from one day to the next. Some have not only brought over their own pain but the pain of others. They are holding their spouse's pain, their mother's problems, their children's concern, their co-worker's hurts, and they have become loaded down with other people's offences. My brother and sister, you are not built to carry so much weight, and definitely not from one day to the next; I don't believe any of us are. We are commanded in Scripture "To lay aside both the weight and the sin that so easily besets us." Could this be why you struggle to sleep at night? Then when you wake, you're tired from wrestling with issues all night because although you may have slept, you did not rest. It's not supposed to be like this.

> *"You'll never know how strong your heart is until you learn to forgive those who broke it."*

Without having a psychology degree on my wall, I can tell you that carrying and holding on to past pain is one of the most useless things you can do in life. Nothing beneficial comes from holding on to hurt, anger, hatred or offences. It is hazardous to your health, and you're going to need good health to climb to the heights of where God wants to take you.

Allow me to pass on some good news. I have some information that will save you money. You will save money on medicine, vitamins, Doctors' fees, Psychologists' fees, and so much more if you make the decision today to forgive all those who have offended you. Those who you still hold responsible, set them free today; even those who have not even acted as though they're sorry for what they did, let them go too. Make the decision, and You will feel younger, lighter, and happier, and you will be fulfilling God's command to forgive.

A common struggle

Then the contention became so sharp that they parted
from one another. And so Barnabas took Mark and
sailed to Cyprus; but Paul chose Silas and departed,
being commended by the brethren to the grace of God.

(Acts 15:39-40 NKJV)

Second to Jesus himself, the apostle Paul is my favourite leader in the Bible. He was one of the most influential leaders of the early church. God used him to spread the gospel to the Gentiles (non-Jews) during the first century, and his missionary journeys took him throughout the Roman empire. A preacher, teacher and counsellor, Paul was remarkable and an excellent example of how a saint is supposed to be. He was trusted and used by God to write half of the books in the New Testament. With such credentials, it may surprise you to learn that Paul, like many of us, struggled with forgiveness too. Paul was disappointed in a particular individual and wouldn't let the issue go.

We read Paul's writing in Philippians 3:13 "Brethren, I count not myself to have apprehended: but this one thing I do, forgetting those things which are behind, and reaching forth unto those things which are before." But when he penned those words, he was not talking about forgetting past hurts, he was alluding to all the things he had achieved, all his successes, all his victories. He confirmed this in Philippians 3:8 when he wrote, "Yea doubtless, and I count all things but loss for the excellency of the knowledge of Christ Jesus my Lord: for whom I have suffered the loss of all things, and do count them but dung, that I may win Christ." Paul indeed achieved much but when it came to forgiveness, Acts chapter 15 lets us know that Paul had a struggled just like you and me.

History of hurt

In Acts 7, Steven was stoned to death, he became the first Christian martyr, and when the Jews stoned Stephen, it caused panic among the other disciples of Jesus. They began to flee to other cities to escape a similar fate. They went to cities such as Cyprus, Cyrene, Antioch and others to escape possible persecution and preach the good news of the Gospel. History tells us that it was in Antioch, where the Gospel began to thrive. It grew exponentially. Sinners became believers, gentiles too were converted, and we are told that it was in Antioch that the disciples were first called Christians.

Because the growth of the Gospel was so rapid in that city, the apostles in Jerusalem sent help to those in Antioch. Barnabas was one of the first sent, and when he arrived and saw the growth and success, he reported back to Jerusalem that they needed additional help. Barnabas prayed about this, and after praying, he decided that Paul was the one needed. Paul, at the time, was in Tarsus, so Barnabas travelled to Tarsus to get Paul. When they returned, Barnabas and Paul partnered together to pastor this thriving church in Antioch.

Whilst Barnabas and Paul were in Antioch, a prophet called Agabus arrived to inform them about a famine that was taking place in Jerusalem, that on hearing this, they became so concerned about the church back in Jerusalem. They collected a love offering from the church in Antioch to aid Jerusalem, and both Barnabas and Paul delivered the love offering to Jerusalem. After providing the love offering, they returned to Antioch, but this time they brought a young man named John Mark, and so now they had become a trio in ministry.

By the time you get to Acts chapter 13, while in the middle of a prayer meeting, the Holy Spirit spoke and told the church to separate Paul and Barnabas from the rest because God has a particular assignment for them. The Holy Spirit ordained Paul and Barnabas to leave Antioch and sail to other cities to preach the Gospel, and the Bible says that they took John Mark with them.

The Holy Spirit was sending them to many places to preach the good news of Jesus Christ. The first stop on their journey was a town called Pathos. The moment they arrived; they had an unpleasant experience with a sorcerer named Elymas (also known as Bar Jesus). Although things got bad and there was tension, Paul and Barnabas worked it out, and they had great success. Then they sailed to an island called Pamphylia. When they arrived, John Mark whom, they had brought along, decided to quit. They had only been to one city, and they only had one issue, but John Mark said, "I quit," and he returned to Jerusalem. However, Paul and Barnabas continued on their journey and went to Pisidia, Iconium, Lystra and Derbe, preaching the good news.

When this first missionary journey was over, they returned to Jerusalem to debate with the rest of the apostles concerning the necessity of circumcision. When the debate ended, the Holy Spirit told Paul to return to those cities to ensure everything was still developing well. Paul relayed this message to Barnabas, and Barnabas replied, "Ok, let's tell John Mark."

Paul insisted that John Mark would in no way be returning with them because Paul had not forgotten how John Mark quit on them during the first journey in Acts 13. Paul was adamant that this time John Mark would not travel with them on this second trip. Barnabas, however, continued to fight on John Mark's behalf, causing much tension between the two, but Paul too was adamant.

Paul and Barnabas argued so vehemently over John Mark that they parted ways because Paul would not forget or forgive John Mark for what he had done. Consequently, that day Paul lost Barnabas, his partner in ministry with whom he had previously worked so well and enjoyed great success.

When I first read this, it left me quite disturbed. It was devastating because both Paul and Mark were Christians. Mark has a Gospel named after him, and Paul wrote half of the New Testament books. Many would think that if any two people ought to be able to work together, it would be Paul and Barnabas, but because Paul refused to forgive John Mark and let it go, the ministry suffered. Paul and Barnabas broke up over this issue, and they never worked together again.

After this break-up, you never hear about Barnabas again, which means Paul probably was never reconciled to Barnabas. This brings home a sad reality that some relationships may never be restored to what they were before if forgiveness isn't granted.

To withhold forgiveness keeps alive emotions of hurt, anger and blame. You remain a victim, and you continue to suffer by holding on to pain and resentment because sorrow intensifies as you keep it alive. It has been proven that there is such a close association between illness and negative emotions. If you were to step up and look at forgiveness from a greater perspective, even though forgiving a perpetrator seems to go against a moral code, in actuality, it aids your emotional welfare. Forgiveness may not change the past, but it does broaden the future.

Time, a true healer

When you read Paul's second letter to Timothy, you will notice by the things Paul says that he does not have long left to live. He knows he has run his race and finished his course. So, in this

> "Forgiveness is a gift you give yourself."
>
> TONY ROBBINS

letter to Timothy, his son in the Gospel, he tells him, "Demas has forsaken me, having loved this present world, and has departed for Thessalonica, Crescens for Galatia, Titus for Dalmatia. Only Luke is with me. Get Mark and bring him with you, for he is useful to me for ministry" (2 Tim. 4:10 KJV).

Notice how Paul broke up with Barnabas, and they are never reconciled, but Paul wants to see John Mark again in his dying days. Paul now wants to restore the relationship that was broken in Acts 15 now that he is getting ready to die. Why now? Why does Paul want John Mark to visit him now in his dying days? What has happened? Some people have suggested it was merely time, that an extended amount of time had passed since the offence and that sometimes reconciliation takes time. Still, why wait until you are about to leave this earth to forgive and reconcile? You can miss out on so much by holding on to hurt and the mistake of others. Let it go, forgive the wrong, free yourself and walk into better possibilities.

The power of forgiveness

Nelson Mandela, played by actor Morgan Freeman in the 2009 film Invictus, declared to the African National Congress in a show of defiance, "Forgiveness starts here... Forgiveness liberates the soul... It removes fear; that is why it is such a powerful weapon. The past is the past, and we look to the future." Some offences are so much more difficult to forgive than others. For example, instances of child abuse or infidelity can be some of the most challenging offences to forgive, yet God instructs us to forgive and let Him deal with the offender.

It's important to understand that forgiving does not mean we're making light of the wrongdoing or devaluing the pain we feel.

Earlier on, I told you that forgiveness is not the natural response for people when they have been hurt. There is something in us that wants to get our own back, and we feel that letting it go is only benefitting the offender, but forgiveness, although it may benefit the perpetrator significantly, it doesn't benefit them nearly as much as it benefits us.

Despite how illogical it may seem; it is only through unconditional forgiveness that we can get over the past and embrace a future feeling totally freed. This practice of Forgiveness opens the window and exposes our wounds to the light, and by exposing those wounds to the light, our suffering is healed.

Forgiveness and Its frequency

As I close this chapter, I want to deal with a question that has been asked by many who have been on the receiving end of an offence. The apostle Peter asked the same question, "Lord, how many times shall I forgive my brother or sister who sins against me - up to seven times?" Peter's question is not an unreasonable question, "How many times do I have to forgive someone who has done me wrong?" a business partner who never pulls his weight, a spouse who has cheated, a parent who has failed to keep their word yet again, a friend who has betrayed me, how many times? Is seven times sufficient?

When Peter asked this question, he thought he was suggesting a great number. In his eyes, seven was more than enough chances to give an offender. Jesus answered, "I tell you, not just seven times, but seventy times seven." Can you imagine the look of horror on

Peter's face? This was much more than what he had imagined, and to make it worse, when you read this story in Luke's Gospel, Jesus says, "Even if he sins against you seven times in a day, and seven times returns to say, 'I repent,' you must forgive him." So, this number can be viewed as the daily number for offering forgiveness. It becomes a necessity because living in unforgiveness and bitterness is to live in a mental prison. It incarcerates you and cuts you off from the brightness of a much better future.

I need to remind you that no matter how much pain or hurt you're struggling with, no one cares more or is more upset about it than the Lord Himself, and He promises to deal with the offender Himself. "Vengeance is mine saith the Lord; I will repay" (Rom. 12: 19 KJV). God requires that you forgive. As much as this is sometimes difficult to do, even if you forgive in sheer obedience to the word of the Lord, you will experience amazing freedom.

I want to end with this statement, "Forgiveness is a decision." Once you've made it and confessed it, God goes to work on your behalf. Sometimes even after you utter the words "I forgive you," you may still feel the hurt of the offence, but that does not mean you haven't forgiven them. Once you seek to forgive and utter the words, God goes to work, and it will only be a matter of time before the pain subsides.

Your future depends on your willingness to let it go. When you forgive, you heal, and when you let go, you grow. This journey that you're on and where God is taking you is far too important to be grounded by unforgiveness. So, make that decision today. Think about that offender and utter these three words, "I FORGIVE YOU." When you do this, you remove the obstacle to a better life.

*"Holding a grudge doesn't make you strong; it makes you bitter.
Forgiving doesn't make you weak; it sets you free."*

DAVE WILLIS

"Yield not to temptation, for yielding is sin
Each victory will help you or some others to win
Fight manfully onward, dark passions subdue
Look ever to Jesus and He'll carry you through."

AL L. GREEN

7

Made Better from Temptation

*"No temptation has overtaken you except what is
common to mankind. ... God is faithful, and he will
not let you be tempted beyond your ability, but
with the temptation he will also provide the way
of escape, that you may be able to endure it."*

(1 Cor. 10:13)

Temptation is a part of life; you will hardly go one day without being tempted to do something. Somebody once said "Opportunity may knock only once but temptation leans on the doorbell." Merriam Webster dictionary defines temptation as "Something that causes a strong urge or desire to have or do something and especially something bad, wrong, or unwise." It is interesting to note the use of the words "a strong urge" because that is exactly what it is. Sometimes it feels like everything in you wants it and must have it or do it and it is always presented so well. In those moments, remember free cheese is always available in mouse traps. The devil rarely comes dressed in a red cape and pointy horns; he comes disguised as everything you've ever wished for. But the good news is you have power over him; and you can always overcome his temptation, there is always a way out. God, in His word, has promised never to allow a temptation to come your way that he hasn't given you the strength to handle. You are stronger than you know.

When temptation knocks, imagination usually answers. I have often said, the mind is the battlefield where temptation is fought. This battle of sin can be won or lost in the mind. Temptation begins with a thought; and if you can control or deal with your thoughts, you can neutralise the lure of temptation. When these bad thoughts enter your head, replace them with better thoughts, remember "Whatsoever things are lovely, whatsoever things are true, honest, and pure, whatsoever things are lovely and of good report, think on these things (Phil. 4:8 KJV).

> *"Satan's chief tactic is deception and he does it by telling people lies about God."*
>
> C. PETER WAGNER

The fastest way to combat temptation is to turn your attention and focus on something else. If you are serious about defeating temptation, you must manage your mind. Interestingly, Paul says, "Let this mind be in you that was also in Christ Jesus" (Phil. 2:5 KJV). It is possible for us to have the same mind that Christ had; by this, I mean the same attitude.

Jesus, too was tempted in his mind. Remember that just like you and I, Jesus could have succumbed to the temptation. He was capable of sinning, yet he didn't. If He did surrender, He would have thwarted the plan of salvation, but he resisted, and he remained steadfast. Had there been no possibility of his yielding to Satan's enticement, then there wouldn't have been a real test, and therefore no genuine victory in the result. The Bible says, "He was in all points tempted like as we are, yet without sin" (Heb. 15 KJV). Let's for a minute look at three areas in which He was tempted.

The Bible says that Jesus was led by the Spirit into the wilderness to be tempted by the devil. Before Jesus commenced his ministry and embarked upon the most extraordinary task that would ever be accomplished in this world, He had to experience temptation. The Bible says that he was led into the wilderness to be tempted by the devil. In the wilderness, He fasted so that his mortal body would be entirely under the divine influence of His Father's Spirit.

After completing a forty-day fast, he was hungry and weakened and left to be tempted by the devil. It was part of the preparation. I can tell you from experience that it is at those times when we feel drained, weary and vulnerable, that the devil often strikes.

Satan's first temptation was to get Jesus to satisfy his hunger; a craving for food is the most basic, physical, biological need. This was an appeal of the appetite, a temptation aimed at his senses. One could surmise that it is the most common and most dangerous of the devil's enticements. Satan said, "If thou be the Son of God, command that these stones be made bread" (Matt. 4:3 KJV). Satan was not simply tempting Jesus to eat. Jesus would have eaten after his fast anyway. Satan's temptation was to have Jesus satisfy his flesh, now using his divine powers for selfish purposes. The trick was in his invitation, to miraculously and instantaneously turn stone into bread without waiting or postponing physical gratification. This temptation was deposited in his mind as temptations are. The devil speaks thoughts into minds. Jesus replied, "It is written, Man shall not live by bread alone, but by every word that proceedeth out of the mouth of God" (Matt. 4:4 KJV).

When Satan realised he had failed to get Jesus to use his divine powers for personal gratification, Satan went to the other extreme. He tempted Jesus to throw himself upon the Father's protection. He took Jesus into the Holy City, to the pinnacle of the temple overlooking the courts and people below, and quoted scripture: "If thou be the Son of God, cast thyself down: for it is written, He shall give his angels charge concerning thee: and in their hands, they shall bear thee up, lest at any time thou dash thy foot against a stone" (Matt. 4:6 KJV).

Within this second request of Satan was a temptation of the mortal nature to perform an impressive feat, a breath-taking exploit, which would have amazed crowds. Can you imagine how jumping from the heights of a temple and floating down in the courtyard unhurt before a group of people would be a fantastic accomplishment? It would show everybody that Jesus is some superior being, and can you see how his fame would spread like wildfire? Everybody would believe that the Messiah indeed had come. But this was not how people were to believe in Jesus.

Jesus would later say to Thomas, "Blessed are they who believe though they have not seen (John 20:29 KJV). Our faith and belief in God must be evident before we see miracles of any kind; we don't see miracles to believe; we must believe first. When Satan spoke to Jesus with this suggestion, Jesus said, "It is written again, thou shalt not tempt the Lord thy God" (Matt. 4:7 KJV). Satan once again failed in tempting Jesus.

In his third temptation, Satan shows Jesus all the kingdoms of the world and the glory of them. The cities, the fields, the flocks, the herds, and everything nature could offer and offers them all to Jesus, although they were not his to give. He shows Jesus the splendour, wealth, and earthly glory from a high mountain and says, "All these things will I give thee if thou wilt fall down and worship me" (Matt. 4:9 KJV).

He was subtly saying that everyone has a price. Jesus also knew that if he were faithful to his Father and obedient to every commandment, he would inherit all things anyway. Jesus said, "Get thee hence, Satan: for it is written, thou shalt worship the Lord thy God, and him only shalt thou serve" (Matt. 4:10 KJV). When Satan realised he had failed in his attempt to get Jesus to succumb, the Bible says the devil left him for a season, and angels came and minister to him.

> *"Every moment of resistance to temptation is a victory."*
>
> FREDERICK WILLIAM FABER

With all of these temptations, the devil posed the same question "If you are the son of God." Satan already knew Jesus was the son of God; he heard the father declare this at Jesus' baptism days earlier. Remember, God said, "This is my beloved son in whom I am well pleased," and Satan was there to hear it. Satan tried to plant doubt in Jesus' mind. It is what he does with us when he wants to get us to do something too. In all these temptations, Satan foreshadows what he would use for his final temptation in getting Jesus not to complete his assignment. On the cross three years later: Satan repeated his tactics through the thief hanging beside Jesus on the cross, "If thou be the Son of God, come down from the cross" (Matt. 27:40 KJV). Jesus could have called twelve thousand angels to come and lift him from the cross, but if He had succumbed to Satan's suggestion, salvation would not have come to the world. When you have the mind of Christ, you want to please the father. It is a sacrificial mindset, a serving mindset. It is this mind that Paul says we need to adopt.

Satan is after your mind. He will use anyone or anything to speak to your mind. It reminds me of two ladies who had lived next door to each other for many years. One lady rose at three o'clock in the morning and looked through her window and saw that her neighbour was in the kitchen. Later that day, she asked, "What were you doing up at three o'clock this morning?" The neighbour responded, "I was cooking for my husband; he had just gotten home." "So you got up at three o'clock to cook for your husband?" The nosey neighbour asked and continued, "I would never get up at three o'clock to cook for anybody." The wife then responded, "I love my husband, and I would get up at any time to cook for him." This shows the kind of thing love will do; it sacrifices.

What if she allowed her neighbour to influence her to stop doing the very thing that made her marriage so successful? We have to be mindful when listening to others who want to tell us what we should and should not be doing. You might just be listening to the devil himself. If you are serious about defeating temptation, you must manage your mind and who you allow to influence it. Choose carefully who you listen to and what you think about. Be very selective.

Another way of overcoming temptation is to acknowledge your struggle and be willing to disclose it. You cannot tell everybody what you are struggling with because some people are judgemental and not trustworthy. Still, if you can find that special brother or sister, that special friend to whom you can be accountable, that person can also help you pray. James tells us, "Therefore confess your sins to each other and pray for each other so that you may be healed. The prayer of a righteous person is powerful and effective" (James 5:16 NIV).

Sometimes, what is killing us is our secret struggles. We are struggling, and because we feel we can't tell anybody, we enclose ourselves in prisons of guilt and shame. Listen, that temptation you are wrestling with is not uniquely yours; others have wrestled with it too. We all have sinned and come short of the glory of God (Rom. 3:23 KJV). God's intention is for you to confess it, don't conceal it but reveal it. Take off the mask; you don't have to pretend to be faultless. God has forgiven you already. He did that on the Cross of Calvary, but when you expose the sin or temptation, you no longer suffer in silence.

> *"Let him who is without sin cast the first stone."*
>
> JESUS OF NAZARETH

It has been said that problems that grow in the dark become more prominent, but they shrink when exposed to the light of truth. There is something about confessing that brings liberation and relief. It is like a pressure valve releasing what has been trapped. The devil cannot secretly threaten you with something you are willing to expose. I know to speak it and release it can make you feel vulnerable, and it is a humbling experience but remember God shows favour to the humble (Prov. 3:34 KJV).

When the woman that was caught in adultery was brought to Jesus, in John 7:53, it was the best thing that could have happen to her because her sin and shortcomings were exposed, and notice what Jesus said, and how he said it, "Woman where are your accusers; does no one accuse you? Nor do I, go and sin no more."

Spiritual Warfare

A powerful aid in overcoming temptation is to have the correct understanding of spiritual warfare. Spiritual warfare is the term used to describe this spiritual battle that we face. This battle is real and shouldn't be ignored. So is the armour and weapons that God has already given you. The book of Ephesians gives us much-needed information about spiritual warfare. The first three chapters of Ephesians explains our position in Christ. It describes how we've been seated with Christ in heavenly places. Ephesians chapters four and five describe how we're to walk and live as followers of Jesus. Ephesians six is the conclusion that describes how we're to stand in the face of temptation and opposition.

"God never said the weapons wouldn't form, He said they wouldn't prosper."

Paul says in Ephesians 6:11-13, "Put on the whole armour of God that ye may be able to stand against the wiles of the devil; for we wrestle not against flesh and blood, but against principalities, against powers, against the rulers of the darkness of this world, against spiritual wickedness in high places. Wherefore take unto you the whole armour of God, that ye may be able to withstand in the evil day, and having done all, to stand."

To put on this armour, you need to be aware of the spiritual blessings God has already given. Every piece of the armour serves a different purpose in protecting you, so to be fully protected, you need to put on the whole armour of God.

The very first step is to accept God's salvation. You won't be able to say no to the devil unless you say yes to Christ. Then you can put on the armour of God, believing what God has done for you through Jesus Christ. And then by living out the elements of the armour in every area of your life, you will be able to overcome all the schemes of the devil.

The devil knows how to attack you, and he doesn't believe in fighting fair. The whole armour of God will protect you from any kind of guilt, doubt, fear and accusation he throws in your direction. We all get tempted in these areas and others, but we are overcomers in Christ.

I always feel the need to remind my church that temptation is not wrong; being tempted is a part of our Christian experience. Jesus too, was tempted in all points yet without sin. It is the yielding to it that makes it wrong. Understanding this removes a weight from your shoulders. You don't have to feel dirty because you were tempted, you are still righteous in spite of the temptation.

Belt of Truth

Let's consider the first piece of the armour of God mentioned in Ephesians six. Paul tells us to stand firm, with the belt of truth buckled around your waist. Notice it is an armour of truth, fact and reality. This is put on when you say: "I believe all that the Bible says about what Jesus did for me. I refuse to believe the lies of the enemy. I gird myself with the truth." When you know the truth, you will recognise the counterfeit. My friend, God has given you every spiritual blessing in the heavenly places in Christ (Eph. 1:3 KJV). It says that you've been raised with Christ and seated with Him; that you've been chosen, adopted, redeemed, forgiven, and sealed with the Holy Spirit (Eph. 3: 1-14 KJV). Do you see how wonderful that truth is?

We often feel the weight of guilt and shame, especially when we fall to the same sin again? But you need to know that God accepts you because of what Jesus has already done for you, and yes, you may have fallen but get up again. A righteous man falls seven times but gets up again (Prov. 24:16 KJV). Will you believe God's truth? Jesus has already paid the price for the penalty of your sin. If you believe God's truth, then you'll be able to stand against the wiles of the enemy. It will be like a belt that supports you so that you can stand.

Breastplate of Righteousness

It shouldn't surprise anyone that soldiers needed to wear a breastplate going into a battle. It protected vital organs secured by a belt, which we discussed earlier. The breastplate of righteousness is what protects the core of your being against every spiritual attack. It covers what's closest to your heart. It affects how you feel about yourself at the heart-level. It affects whether you walk in confidence as someone secure in knowing that God loves them and stops you from trying to earn God's favour in your life because you know you are already blessed and highly favoured.

Righteousness is a gift that has been given to you once you have accepted Jesus Christ into your life. It is provided to you by God, our Father, and it is something you could never achieve by yourself. All our righteousness is as filthy rags (Isa 64:6 KJV). This righteousness, and perfection, comes to us through Jesus' death and resurrection on the cross. Jesus took our place by living the life we should live and dying the death we deserve to die. When he rose, He justified us and offered a covering of righteousness.

You put on the breastplate of righteousness by trusting in what God has done for you in Jesus. He has chosen us to be holy and without blame before Him in love, entirely

"An unopened gift is worthless."

accepted by Him through His Beloved, Son Jesus. So, we can boldly say: "I no longer have to trust my own goodness. It doesn't come from good works. It matters not how much community service I do. It matters not how often I attend church or how often I read the

Bible. I trust Jesus to be righteous for me." When you know that God accepts you and enjoys you because of what Jesus did, you are wearing the breastplate of Righteousness.

Peaceful Feet

The third part of the armour deals with our feet. We must be equipped and able to stand against any spiritual attack. Our feet are to be shod with the Gospel of peace. The word Peace is #7965 in Strong's concordance and it is written as שָׁלוֹם and pronounced (shaw-lome). Shalom is more than just simply peace; it is a complete peace. It is a feeling of contentment, completeness, soundness, tranquillity, wholeness, health, well-being and harmony. This is where God says he will keep us if we keep our minds stayed on him, because we trust in Him (Isaiah 26:3 KJV).

Peace is one of the most potent weapons we have. The enemy doesn't know what to do with someone who lives in peace and refuses to be hassled. The reason we can enjoy such peace is because God has done the utmost in reconciling us to Himself through Christ (2 Cor. 5:18). We are now His ambassadors. We now have a responsibility to take the message of God's peace to the people so that they can have it too.

Our shoes are of peace because God's peace is made available to us through what Jesus, the Prince of Peace, did on the cross in dying for sin. The sin that separated people from God has been paid for by Jesus. We can now have both peace with God and have the peace of God. Reconciliation with God has been achieved. When you have your feet shod with the Gospel of peace, there is a readiness and willingness to go wherever the Lord sends you, regardless of how worthless you are made to feel by the devil.

In his epistle to the elect pilgrims, the apostle Peter said, "But sanctify the Lord God in your hearts, and always be ready to give a defence to everyone who asks you a reason for the hope that is in you, with meekness and fear" (1 Peter 3:15 KJV). This part of the armour is there as encouragement because when times get hard, we are still required to share the good news of the Gospel. Even through times of discouragement and persecution, you can still stand with peace to do God's will.

Shield of Faith

Paul said, "In addition to all this, take up the shield of faith, with which you can extinguish all the flaming arrows of the evil one". The English Standard Version puts it this way, "In all circumstances, take up the shield of faith, with which you can extinguish all the flaming darts of the evil one" (Eph. 6:16 ESV). A shield is vitally important to a soldier. It provides a blanket of protection. It is meant to be taken up in all circumstances. It is the first barrier against the enemy's attack.

The Roman shield of that time was called a scutum. It was nearly as large as a door and would cover the warrior entirely. It was not just defensive but could also be used to push opponents. It was also effective when fighting as a group because a group of soldiers could position their shields to form an enclosure around themselves, called a testudo ("tortoise"). They would help significantly to protect them against arrows launched from the city walls. These shields were often made of wood and then covered in hide. This way, when they got wet, they could effectively extinguish the flaming arrows hurled by the enemy.

According to this text, the shield of faith is the part of the armour of God that protects you from the flaming darts of the enemy. As you know, the devil has darts that he lets loose on God's people - darts such as accusations and threats. The Bible says Satan is the accuser of the brethren. He will accuse you before God and each other but he is liar and the father of lies. The onslaught of darts that the enemy sends is to destabilise you but the shield of faith will protect you.

Faith is how we started our walk with God, by believing in Jesus. We were saved by grace through faith. It is also how we progress in our spiritual growth and faith is what will help you keep standing until the end, when you stand before Jesus, the founder and perfecter of our faith (Heb. 12:2 ESV).

It is no wonder the enemy will try to attack our faith because faith is the bedrock, the substratum; if the enemy can destroy that, he can destroy you. He will come to shake your belief in God's Word, your belief in God's love for you, and in His plans for your life. He comes to shake your confidence in God.

Satan's attacks can sometimes cause us to doubt God. He tries to cause our faith to waver. Don't ever be tempted to believe what he is offering is better than what God has promised. When Satan attempts to plague us with doubt or entice us with instant gratification, faith recognizes the deceptiveness of his tactics and quickly extinguishes the arrows. That shield of faith is imperative when fighting the enemy. Though your feelings and your mind may change from time to time, your faith must not be shaken. To take up the shield of faith means to put your personal trust in God in every circumstance.

Faith is a protective barrier between us and the schemes of Satan. When you take up the shield of faith, and hold it tightly, you grasp firmly to your Saviour, your Commander and Chief, who is the author and finisher of our faith.

Helmet of Salvation

The Roman helmet, known as a galea, varied in design because each helmet was created individually. Usually, the helmets were made of metal, though poorer soldiers may have had leather helmets fortified with metal pieces. The most obvious value of the helmet was to protect against blows to the head. Helmets usually had cheek plates to guard against blows to the face and a metal piece in the back to protect against impacts to the back of the neck.

We, as Christians, are soldiers on the battlefield for our Lord. The helmet of Salvation protects a soldier against damaging and deadly blows to the head. It provides hope and protects the mind against anything that would disorientate it or destroy it, such as discouragement and deceit. I said earlier that the mind is one of the most vulnerable organs and has to be protected. What goes into the mind and remains can control that person. The helmet of Salvation reminds us of the truth that God is the One who saves; it is our guarantee. When you wear it, you are confident in your Salvation and where you will spend eternity. When Christians mislay their helmets, it's like they are "hoping" to be saved; that kind of "hoping to be saved" is not useful at all. It won't do you much good when the conflict grows fierce.

Hope is never a vague optimism that everything will work out in the end, but it is a settled conviction. We can know for sure that we are saved, and we're going to heaven. The apostle John says, "I write these things to you who believe in the name of the Son of God, that you may know that you have eternal life" (1 John 5:13 KJV).

John wants us to know for sure we're going to heaven, and he explains how: "This is the testimony, that God gave us eternal life, and this life is in His Son. Whoever has the Son has life; whoever does not have the Son of God does not have life" (1 John 5:11–12 KJV). The helmet of salvation is our sure hope. Eternal life is God's gift, which comes to us wrapped up in His Son. If we have Jesus, we have life. If we don't have Jesus, we don't have life. Thank God for Jesus.

So, the Gospel is that he died and was buried, but He also rose again. And Jesus will return at the end of this age to bring God's Kingdom fully on the earth (Revelation 21-22). Sin has caused this world to be in a state of brokenness. Gross darkness will continue to increase until Jesus returns. The hope for the child of God is that we won't be left in this world to suffer much longer; our salvation brings us hope. You put on this helmet of salvation when you place your hope, fully in God. He started the work of redemption and will one day complete it. The apostle John says, "He that has this hope in him purifies himself even as he is pure" (1 John 3:3 KJV). As we endeavour to keep ourselves pure, God is pleased, but even when we fail, the helmet of salvation reminds us that we are still saved with tremendous hope.

Sword of the Spirit

This last part of the armour is the sword of the spirit which is the Word of God. Whilst the other parts of the armour are defensive, this part is offensive. Hebrews 4:12 also describes the Word of God as a two-edged sword. "For the word of God is living and active, sharper than any two-edged sword, piercing to the division of soul and of spirit, of joints and of marrow, and discerning the thoughts and intentions of the heart" (Heb. 4:12 KJV). All the armour pieces come from God, but this piece, in particular, is God himself. It's Logos, the same Word used to describe God in John 1:1.

But we must know how to properly wield a sword for maximum effect. If we misuse the sword of the Spirit, we'll put ourselves in danger on the spiritual battlefield. Whether using the Word of God for the offensive (evangelism efforts), defensive (apologetics), or to war against Satan himself (battle), we need to know it to be able to use it properly. Earlier I showed you Jesus, using it when tempted by the devil in the wilderness. He wielded it to great effect. This weapon is two-edged; indeed, razor-sharp in every way, whichever way it strikes, it is effective, beware how you handle it!

One of the worst ways to use your sword is to read it out of context or read into it your own cultural biases. To avoid this misuse, we need to study daily, read commentaries and hear sermons preached on the Word to understand Scripture. I stress this because as you interact with people, you will come in contact with believers of other religions and atheists, who will often twist Scripture. We must always be ready to give an answer to these challenging questions that will most certainly arise. This is what Philip was able to do with the Ethiopian eunuch in Acts 8:26. This eunuch was reading a portion of Scripture he didn't understand. Philip, however, being a follower of Jesus, was in the area and was used by the Holy Spirit to explain the Scripture to him, leading the man to salvation.

We are supposed to be able to explain Scripture to those who don't understand it. As we spend time in God's Word every day, not only do we learn more about him and grow closer to him, but we arm ourselves for victory. This excellent book, which contains the utterances of God's mouth, is the one weapon that the Holy Ghost elects to use for his warlike purposes. He can make a man feel the divine power of the sacred Word in the very centre of his being. It is "the sword of the spirit" because he alone can instruct us in the use of it. This piece of armour has many benefits, and it is effective in nullifying the power of temptation.

Reality Check

I close this chapter bringing you into the realisation that everyone of us is vulnerable. We are warned never to be over confident and never to get cocky. In short don't fool yourself.

Don't be so naive and self-confident. You're not exempt. You could fall flat on your face as easily as anyone else. Forget about self-confidence; it's useless. Cultivate God-confidence.

(1 Cor 10:12 MSG)

My friend, we are fighting an experienced enemy who has practised his craft since he was kicked out of heaven. He knows what made you fall the last time; he knows what made your parents and grandparents fall, and he will try it on you too. Therefore, we should never allow our guard to come down because, given the right circumstance and being in the wrong environment can make anyone capable of yielding to temptation and falling into sin. So, we must avoid placing ourselves in tempting situations. Don't hang around with that person, don't go to that house alone, don't watch that seductive program; don't drink that alcoholic drink. I have found it easier to stay out of temptation than to get out of temptation. God will always make a way of escape but staying far away from it is the best option.

When Jesus overcame his temptation in the wilderness, the Bible says angels came and ministered to him. You have angels waiting to minister to you too. They are on hand to help when you say no to the devil's temptation. So, fight with all your might. The devil goes around like a roaring lion seeking whom he may devour, but you can be victorious. You are more than a conqueror, and angelic help is on hand.

Blessed is the man, that endureth temptation; for when he is tried, he shall receive the crown of life.

JAMES 1:12

"Prayer is the most important conversation of your day.
Take it to God before you to take it to anyone else."

8

You Can Do Better Things

After Jesus had gone indoors, his disciples asked him privately, "Why couldn't we drive it out?" He replied, "This kind can come out only by prayer."

(Mark 9:28 NIV)

At the time of writing this chapter, our country and much of the world faces one of the greatest challenges ever seen in our generation. People are losing their minds; the mental health of many is at risk of breaking down. The latest statistics from one source states that there has been a 183% rise in mental health cases in the last few months alone. This has all occurred because of the coronavirus. Covid 19 has ravished much of the country and the world. Whoever thought with our technology and our advancement in medicine that a virus could be so devastating, taking the lives of so many people?

As of this moment, according to 'worldometers.info', the death count in the UK stands at 98,531. France has a death count of

73,494, Spain 56,208, Italy 85,881, Mexico 150,273, and the USA has the highest count being 431,392. Every country has a count in the thousands, and as you can see, some in the hundreds of thousands. To date, the total world count of deaths caused by this virus is a horrific 2,151,569 (two million, one hundred and fifty-one thousand, five hundred and sixty-nine) people.

The Bible tells us in Tim. 3:1, In the last days, perilous time will come. Men will be lovers of themselves. Lovers of money. Boastful, arrogant, abusive, disobedient to their parents. Ungrateful, unholy without love, unforgiving, slanderous, without self-control. Brutal, not lovers of the good, treacherous, rash, conceited, lovers of pleasure rather than lovers of God. It makes you question; can times get any more perilous than what they are right now? Who knows what challenges the rest of the year will bring? But for the Christian, there is one way in which we are told to face every challenge, which is guaranteed to bring us success, and that is by having a communicative relationship with God.

Any successful relationship involves communication, whether it be a business relationship, a personal relationship, a marital relationship or a social relationship. If it's going to be successful at all, good communication is essential. Communication, however, is not just the ability to speak, because you can talk to somebody for an hour and still not communicate a thing because they haven't understood a word you've been saying. Communication is more of the ability to be understood. For communication to be successful, transmitting and receiving has to be accomplished. When people really know each other, they can sometimes communicate without even speaking words, just a look and the other person knows what they're saying, just a smile and the other person knows what they're thinking. So, relationships are successful when communication is successful, and if we are to have a successful personal relationship with God, communication with God is essential; that's why prayer is vital.

Prayer is not just speaking; it is entering into the presence of God, once in His presence, even when you can't find the words to say, your very groan can be understood and interpreted by God. Your tears, too. Prayer then is not so much what you say but what is understood.

Something happens when a child of God prays. A divine exchange takes place. God hears their cry and, in turn, replies. God sees their needs and in turn supplies. That's why the writer of the Hebrews tells us in Heb. 4:15 that we have not a high priest which cannot be touched with the feeling of our infirmities; but was in all points tempted like as we are, yet without sin. Christ, our high priest, is able to empathise with our infirmities. He feels how we feel at that most profound level.

The next verse tells us that Christ can empathise, which is why we need to pray. Let us, therefore, come boldly unto the throne of grace, that we may obtain mercy and find grace to help in time of need (Heb. 4:16). This challenge we are facing is indeed a time of need. We've never seen it like this before. Nurses have to do video calls in front of dying patients so that loved ones can say their goodbyes. Funeral homes are overrun. Companies are deleting jobs and laying people off, many of which will not recover. Families are going hungry; people are begging in the streets. Marriages are breaking up because of a pressure they cannot bear; we are living in a time of need. And when we come boldly to God in prayer, that's when God pours out wisdom & strength for the challenge; that's when God pours out anointings for the yoke because it is the anointing that breaks the yoke. Prayer has to be the lifestyle of the Christian during this time.

If we don't pray, does it mean that we are still saved? Yes we are. If we don't pray, does it mean we are still going to heaven? Yes, we are. "We are saved by grace through faith; and that not of yourselves: it is the gift of God: not of works, lest any man should boast" (Eph. 2:8-9). So then, our salvation has already been taken care of. In fact, Eph. 1:13 tells us that when we heard the word of truth, the gospel of salvation, and believed in him, we were sealed with the promised Holy Spirit. So, our salvation is sure, but if we don't pray, we become powerless Christians. We become weak and impotent Christians that will succumb to any kind of challenge. That's why Jesus said: "Watch and pray so that you don't enter into temptation, for the spirit is willing, but the flesh is weak" (Matt 26:41). So prayer has to be our lifestyle. It has to be our daily practise.

> *"When prayer becomes your habit, miracles become your lifestyle."*

Too busy to pray

Some of you may be thinking: I really do want to pray more often, but I don't have the time. Listen! The busier you are, the more you need to pray. The devil will try to keep you so busy, knowing that once he stops you from praying, he cuts your communication and fellowship off with God. Once your communication and fellowship are cut, your gifts are not as sharp, your discernment is off, and you won't even be able to discern when the enemy is sending his demon. Before you know it, the devil has come and robbed you of your joy, robbed you of your peace, robbed you of your relationships, robbed you of your finances, and you'll be left asking: What happened? You didn't pray. You left yourself wide open to his attack; without prayer, we become powerless.

BUSY has been defined in an acronym as Being Under Satan's Yoke. A yoke is a trap he uses to get the better of you. If he can keep you so occupied with stuff and even good stuff that your focus is taken away, he has succeeded.

> *"When you can't put your prayer into words God hears your heart."*

The best way to illustrate this is by likening it to embarking upon a journey by car. Most of us have at some point or another done this. Can you imagine getting on the motor to begin your trip only to discover your fuel light is warning you that you're almost out of fuel? At the same time, you see a sign on the road informing you of a service station five miles down the road. When you travel the five miles and reach the turning for the service station, you foolishly decide that you're in much too much of a hurry to stop now, so you continue driving trying to make it to the next service station that is ten miles further.

After six miles, as you continue pressing the accelerator, you feel the car slowing down. It can no longer continue. It has become powerless due to running out of fuel. Now you're forced to get out of the car and walk miles to a service station carrying a fuel can. So,

99

what you thought you didn't have time to do, you had to find time to do, and in the process, you have done damage to your car by allowing dirt to get into the engine, all the while making yourself even later for your trip. You thought by not stopping, you would save time, but in reality, you wasted time.

Many of us live our lives like this, thinking we can make it through the day, through the week, through the challenge without fuelling up. The problem is that we don't know what is coming our way that day, that week that month or that year. If we are running on empty, before long we will break down because a situation will come our way, that we're not prepared for. This is seen quite clearly in the story recorded in Mark 9.

Jesus and three of his disciples came down from a mountain. When they reached the foot of the mountain, they saw a crowd surrounding the nine disciples that were left behind. The crowd were arguing and debating with them. When the crowd turned and saw Jesus, they came running to him. Then a man in the crowd said to Jesus, "Teacher, I brought you my son, who is possessed by a spirit. It has robbed him of his speech, and whenever it seizes him, it throws him to the ground, causing him to foam at the mouth, gnash his teeth and become rigid. I asked your disciples to drive out the spirit, but they could not." This spirit would enter the child, cause havoc on the child and leave him weak. It would do that repeatedly. After hearing this, Jesus told the father to bring the child to him.

A further lesson is seen in this story. Notice, Jesus didn't tell the father to send the child to him but bring the child. Parents are often content to send their children to Sunday school, youth camp and church, but they don't come themselves. Of course, sending your child to church is good but bringing them to church is better. When you send them to church but stay home yourself, that doesn't set the right example. When you bring them, you show them that God is interested in the whole family's salvation. The Bible says, "Train up a child in the way that he should go and when he is older, he will not depart" (Prov. 22:6). Those teachings will remain with them. The apostle Paul also admonishes us with these words, "Fathers, do not exasperate your children; instead, bring them up in the training and instruction of the Lord" (Eph. 6:4). Bringing your children to Jesus is so much better than just sending them.

When the father brought his son to Jesus, immediately when the demon saw Jesus, he started to tear at the boy causing the boy to fall on the ground and begin foaming at the mouth. As this is happening, Jesus looks at the father and says, how long has he been this way? When Jesus asks a question, it is never because he doesn't know the answer but rather because he wants you to see something.

The father is thinking, please Jesus do something quickly to help my son, but Jesus slows him down with a question. Perhaps Jesus was causing him to think about what took place at the time of the happening. Could it be that Jesus was soliciting an admission or a confession that perhaps the father did something that opened a door for the demon to enter his house in the first place? Parents, we have to be careful what we do and what we get involved in because sometimes our actions can open up doors that should remain closed. Could it be possible that a lifestyle of alcohol abuse, pornography, gambling or something else opened up an avenue for the demon to enter his home? As parents, there are some things we cannot allow in our homes. Perhaps we should be careful about the type of music that is played there too. Some words definitely should not be spoken there because the Bible tells us that "We are snared by the words of our mouth" (Prov. 6:2).

When asked the question, the father replied, "Since he was a child and ofttimes it cast him into the fire, and the waters, to destroy him, but if you can do anything, have compassion on us, and help us." Notice the father's replied, "Help us." Perhaps he realises that he may be part of the cause of the problem. Jesus responded with such encouraging words. "If you can believe, then all things are possible to him that believes." Right then, the father shouts with tears in his eyes, "Lord I do believe, help thou my unbelief."

I think we can all identify with this prayer. Who among us hasn't had to deal with wavering faith; faith that is up and down. I thank God for the power of mustard seed faith. This father's faith was wavering, but it was still enough for God to move on. Jesus rebuked the foul spirit, commanding it to come out of him, and enter into him no more, and at that point, the spirit cried out, tore at him and came out. When the spirit came out, his leaving was not voluntary; it was compulsory. He didn't want to come out, but he had to come out. He exited with a last-minute attempt to remain, tearing at the child so much that many believed he was dead. It was not pretty, but deliverance rarely is. Jesus took the boy by the hand and lifted him.

When the crowd was gone, the nine disciples came to Jesus and said, "Why couldn't we do that?" Why couldn't we drive that demon out of that boy? We've cast demons out before; we know how to do it? They were right. Back in Mark chapter 3, Jesus gave them the power to do it, and in Luke 17:10, they went out and did just that, and came back saying, "Lord even the demons were subject to us in your name."

They were perplexed as to why they could not do it now. Jesus then said something that is key to conquering every challenge: "This kind won't go out except by prayer." My friend, there is a 'this kind' of situation, a 'this kind' of demon that will never move without prayer.

I can image the disciples thinking; this is not fair. How were we to know that we would have to face a 'This kind of situation?' We didn't know this was going to come our way. That is the point exactly. You and I don't know what we're going to come up against and when; that's why it is not enough to pray when the situation comes; we have to be praying all the time. Pray without ceasing. Prayer has got to be your lifestyle so that whatever comes your way during the day, whatever comes your way during the month, or the year, you've already stored up in power through prayer to deal with it.

Jesus leads by example

Jesus modelled this point further in Matthew 26 when he was preparing for his greatest challenge. The same three disciples who he took up to the mountain, he now takes into the Garden of Gethsemane. While there, he confides in them and tells them how he is feeling at that very moment. "My soul is exceedingly sorrowful even unto death." After this admission, he says to them, "Will you watch with me for one hour?" then he goes deeper into the Garden and begins to pray.

It is interesting to note that Jesus always prayed before challenges. He prayed before multiplying the fish and bread when feeding the five thousand. He prayed before raising Lazarus from the dead, and now when about to face His greatest challenge, knowing He will suffer and experience a horrific ordeal to bring salvation to the world, He prays again. Only this time, the intensity was at its highest. The Bible says, "He prayed until his sweat fell like drops of blood" (Luke 22:44).

After praying, he returned to his disciple only to find them asleep; they couldn't keep up with the pace. They couldn't even stay awake with Jesus for one hour. This request for them to stay awake and watch with him happened three times, and all three times, they failed. Eventually, Jesus prayed, "Not my will but thy will be done." Through prayer, Jesus now had fully prepared himself for his greatest challenge, and he met it and completed it with 100% success. If we want to be successful in facing every challenge, we must follow the example of Jesus and make prayer a priority in our lives. When we acknowledge God in all of our ways, He will direct our path, leading us into doing better things.

9

Better from The Family

*And Jacob begot Joseph the husband of Mary,
of whom was born Jesus who is called
Christ. So, all the generations from Abraham
to David are fourteen generations, from David
until the captivity in Babylon are fourteen
generations, and from the captivity in Babylon
until the Christ are fourteen generations.*

(Mt 1:16–17 KJV)

Being blessed to be a Pastor now for some fifteen years, one of the questions new believers often ask me is, "Why are there four Gospels, and why do they differ so much from each other." One of the most accurate and straightforward answers I can give is that each Gospel writer when telling the story of Jesus was writing to a particular audience and therefore wanted to relay different things about Jesus. John tells us that if all the things that Jesus did were recorded, there wouldn't be enough room to contain all the books.

The Gospel of Luke

It is believed that Luke writes his Gospel aimed toward a gentile audience. Luke is traditionally thought of as one of apostle Paul's travelling companions, and it's undoubtedly the case that the author of Luke was from those Greek cities in which Paul had worked. His Gospel, or should I say, the Gospel, according to Luke, tells of the origins, that is, the birth, ministry, death, resurrection, and ascension of Jesus. Luke himself gives a concise and straightforward description of his Gospel in the opening verses of Acts. He says: "In the first book, O Theophilus, I have dealt with all that Jesus began to do and teach, until the day when he was taken up" (Acts 1:1-2 ESV).

Although Luke himself is not mentioned in his Gospel or the Acts of the Apostles, based on the external and internal evidence, his authorship is virtually indisputable. Luke wanted to give his readers an accurate account of the life and teachings of Jesus. If people knew of the kind and compassionate way in which Jesus met individuals, they could be won by the attractive love of Jesus. Luke possessed a rare ability as a writer, so it is sometimes said that his Gospel is the most appealing of all.

The Gospel of Mark

The placement of Mark's Gospel is of interest because although Mark is the first written of all the Gospels, it is strategically placed second in the New Testament's canonical order. From a historical point of view, it is said that Mark being the oldest of all the Gospels, is the most reliable, one of the reasons being, it is closer in time to the events that it records. In this Gospel, Mark takes time to explain Jewish customs, and his translations of Aramaic expressions suggest that he was writing to Gentile converts, perhaps those living in Rome. He records with much accuracy the main event of the teachings and life of Jesus.

This Gospel is the one that establishes the life of Jesus as a story form. It develops a narrative from his early career through his life's main points and culminates in his death. It is also interesting to note that being the first Gospel written allowed it to be one of the primary sources used to write other Gospels such as Matthew and Luke. Therefore, some of the material content is reproduced in their Gospels too.

The Gospel of John

John's Gospel is the latest written of all biographies of Jesus. The central theme is the divine Logos, the Word that was with God, and that was God. This Logos became flesh and dwelt among men in the person of Jesus of Nazareth. As stated by John himself, this Gospel's purpose is to show that Jesus of Nazareth is Christ, the Son of God and that believers in him might have eternal life.

He doesn't say much about the supernatural birth. He regards Jesus as a human being who possessed actual flesh and blood. The most significant thing about Jesus is that the divine Logos was present in him, and all of the marvellous things that he accomplished were by virtue of God's power.

John records only seven miracles, much less than what is listed in the Synoptic Gospels. Each miracle is then used as an introduction to a discourse. As there are only seven, I will take the time to mention them:

1. The turning of water into wine at a marriage feast in Cana.
2. The healing of a nobleman's son who was at the point of death.
3. The recovery of a man at the sheep-gate pool.
4. The walking on water.
5. The feeding of five thousand.
6. The healing of the man born blind.
7. The raising of Lazarus from the dead.

Each miracle becomes the basis of discourse, for example, when he feeds the five thousand with fish and bread, he says, "I am the bread of life." When he raises Lazarus from the dead, He says, "I am the resurrection and the life." When he heals the man, who was born blind, and his disciple are confused about why he was born that way, John records them asking the question, "Rabbi who sinned, was it this man or his parents?" Jesus responded, "It wasn't this man or his parents who sinned. This happened so that it might display the power of God in his life."

John shows that this story leads to the discourse of Jesus, stating, "I am the light of the world." John's primary concern in this story is not physical sight in place of physical blindness, but rather healing men and women of their spiritual blindness.

John wrote for a very varied crowd that included both Jews and Gentiles. It would explain precisely why John used this vernacular in his Gospel. He wanted to get his point across to both the Jews and the Gentiles (non-Jewish) that Jesus is the Son of God.

The Gospel of Matthew

I have left Mathew's Gospel until last because I wanted to show a crucial point. Although this Gospel was not the first Gospel written, it is regarded as very important and therefore is placed first in the New Testament. Matthew's Gospel contains a lot of material such as Jesus' discourses, stories and sayings, some of which is not seen in other Gospels. Certain characteristics distinguish this Gospel from other Gospels. It falls into five distinct divisions. These divisions show a portion of the narrative concerning Jesus' activities and teachings. Each division seems to end with Matthew writing, "When Jesus had finished saying these things." This five-fold division of Matthew's Gospel corresponds in a general way to the divisions found in various parts of the Old Testament.

Matthew begins with a genealogy of Jesus that traces his ancestry as far back as Abraham. The lineage is traced on Joseph's side, although the author later definitively states that Joseph was not Jesus' biological father. Matthew's intention in writing his Gospel is to show and persuade a Jewish audience that Jesus, who they had crucified, was not just some fake prophet but that he was the legitimate Messiah. To do this, Matthew must convince this Jewish crowd that Jesus is a rightful descendant of David because they knew the Messiah had to be a descendant of David.

After listing the genealogy of Jesus, he states, "So, all the generations from Abraham to David are fourteen generations, from David until the captivity in Babylon is fourteen generations, and from the captivity, in Babylon, until the Christ are fourteen generations." And with fitting and grouping the family tree of Jesus into three segments of fourteen generations, Matthew uses the family tree to prove that Jesus is the rightful Messiah. What Matthew is utilizing in doing this is a tool that Jewish people understood in those days called Gematria. Gematria assigns a numeric value to a letter based upon the letter's placement in the alphabet. Gematria, in English would say that A, B, C, D and E have numeric values 1,2,3,4 and 5, respectively. They would use Gematria to spell out a word using letters with assigned numeric value and then total it up. For example, if I wanted to spell GRACE using Gematria: G=7, R=18, A=1, C=3 and E=5. The total numeric value for Grace would add up to 34.

Now bear in mind in the ancient Hebrew language and alphabet, vowels were not written; all that were written were consonants. So, anytime you spelt the name David in Hebrew, you wouldn't see vowels; therefore, if you remove the vowels, you are left with the three consonants D - V - D, pronounce (Dalet, Vav, Dalet). When you add up Dalet, which is the 4th letter; Vav, which is the 6th letter and Dalet, the 4th letter again, you get the numerical value 14.

When Matthew tries to put the family tree of Jesus into three segments of 14 generations, he uses Gematria to prove to the Jews that Jesus is in David's linage because his family tree matches the three consonants in David's name. Matthew is trying to show that Jesus is in the linage of David and, therefore, must be the Messiah.

Jesus' family tree

What is even more surprising in tracing Jesus' family line, is who Matthew names. He names and includes Jews and Gentiles, the kings, some of whom were massive failures, then Matthew mentions women in Jesus' linage too. It is most unusual because when tracing genealogy in Jewish history, it was never done by including the women. Yet, Matthew includes five women and all of these women whom he names have some sort of sexual scandal attached to their name. There is Tamar, Rahab, Ruth, Bathsheba and Mary.

When Matthew mentions Tamar, it takes us back to Genesis 38, a sexually scandalous story. When he mentions Ruth, this too is a sexually scandalous story as she is mentioned as sliding into Boaz's bed. When he mentions Rahab, the sexual scandal associated with her is that she's a prostitute who runs a brothel in the Promised Land. Next, Matthew mentions Uriah's wife, which refers to Bathsheba and the scandalous story of her and Kind David. His adulterous affair led to him killing Uriah, her husband. Three of the women mentioned are Gentiles, Rahab, Ruth and Tamar, so Matthew dares to mention Gentiles, women and sexual scandal in his Gospel, things the Jews would rather not talk about.

And in the second segment between David and Babylon, some of the kings Matthew list were not good; they failed and led Israel into Babylonian exile. This listing of genealogy is a listing of failures, mistakes, disobedience, and sin. Yet in Jesus, we have a man who makes no mistake, who never failed, who obeyed God even to the point of surrendering his life on a cross. How is it possible for so many people in a family line to be failures and dropouts, yet despite all that negativity and failure, God is still able to produce someone so much better, a person who epitomises success?

John said, "In him was life and the life was the light of men, and the light shineth in darkness; and the darkness comprehended it not" (John 1:4-5). How is it that there can be so much darkness and failure, but yet from within it, light and success can burst forth?

This is a picture of what God wants to do with each one of us. Most of us can list some failure and disappointment in our linage. Most of us can remember negative words that have been spoken over us, but the linage of Jesus is proof enough, showing us that "No weapon formed against us shall prosper, and every tongue which rises against us in judgment we shall condemn. This is the heritage of the servants of the Lord, and their righteousness is from Me," Says the Lord (Isaiah 54:17).

Though Jesus' family tree shows failure and is filled with errors, disobedience, and sin, Jesus is able to decide that failure stops right here with me. With Jesus, there is no more sin, no more disobedience, no more failure. My friend, I want you to see that God has given us the power of declaring whatever was wrong in our family in the past; it stops with me. You can decide unforgiveness stops with me. Addiction of any sort stop with me; abuse and sexual scandal stop with me. Do you see what Matthew shows us through the linage of Jesus? That although negative behaviour has existed and ruled up until now, Positive can still spring forth, and we can be that catalyst of change.

If there is one thing the genealogy of Jesus teaches with clarity, it is the assurance that we can have and do better, that just because others before have failed, I don't have to. I can be the one to have success. Just because others have given up, I can be the one who brings it to completion, I can experience better, I can do better, and I can instil better in those that follow me.

It starts with one

It starts with one, perhaps your whole family has failed, but from a family, God can choose one person and use them to make the difference.

One man chosen from his family stuck out his rod, and the Red Sea opened, allowing the children of Israel to walked across on dry land.

One woman, Esther, chosen from her family, prevented an early Jewish holocaust when she decided, "If I perish, let me perish, but I'm going to see the king."

One man, Abraham, was chosen to leave his family and their erroneous beliefs in many gods; to believe in the one true God and became the father of many nations.

One woman, Rahab, kept the twelve Jewish spies safe by hiding them in her loft, and God used her to become kin to Jesus.

One man, David, became the sweet psalmist of Israel and was declared as being a man after God's own heart.

One woman, Deborah, became the only female judge, inspiring the army of Israel to victory over their Canaanite oppressors.

One man, Martin Luther King Jr., was chosen from his family to become the most visible spokesperson and leader in the Civil Rights movement.

One woman, Rosa Parks, refused to give up her seat on the bus and inspired the leaders of the local black community to organise the Montgomery Bus Boycott in 1955.

It only takes one to make the difference and you can be that one. You can make the difference in your family, in your society and in your world. This is what Mordecai said to Esther, "Who knows if you have come into the kingdom for such a time of this." She was the one for her time; you can be the one for your time; great moments are born from great opportunities. When you say yes to it, better is ahead.

10

Being the Better Person

*Joseph is a fruitful bough even a fruitful bough
by a well; whose branches run over the wall.
The archers have sorely grieved him, and shot
at him, and hated him: But his bow abode in
strength, and the arms of his hands were made
strong by the hands of the mighty God of Jacob.*

(Gen. 49:22-24 KJV)

Not too long ago, a TV programme graced our screens. In reality, it was more of a televised competition; nevertheless, they named it "The world's strongest man." On this program, gathered from all over the world were muscle men doing the extraordinary and performing unusual and challenging tasks to demonstrate their strength. Some of the things they chose to do were quite remarkable, for example, some were lifting ridiculously heavy weights, moving cars, some even had ropes tied around their waist with which they attempted to pull lorries and other heavy loads as they walked. All these undertakings were used to measure their strength because life has erroneously made us believe that a person's true strength is measured by what they can do with the power they possess. Still, I wish to stretch your thinking to consider that a person's real strength is not measured by what they can do with their power, but rather it can be seen by what they choose not to do with the power they possess. That real strength has a power that is under control.

We see this in Jesus' use of the word "meek" in His "Sermon on the Mount," found in Matthew 5. In the fifth verse, He says, "Blessed are the meek for they shall inherit the earth." It is interesting that when you consult many dictionaries, they will interpret the word meek as quiet, gentle, and easily imposed on, submissive, or as someone not willing to argue. This modern English idiom of the expression meek hardly makes it one of the honourable words of life. Nowadays, it carries with it an idea of spinelessness, subservience and mean-spiritedness. It paints the picture of a submissive and ineffective person, but these descriptions and definitions are not entirely correct as to what Jesus was saying.

The word he used in Greek was "praus." The meaning of praus is far more significant. In Greek, praus is one of the great Greek ethical words. This adjective refers to having strength under control. In ancient Greece, they trained warhorses to be meek; they were strong and powerful and willing to submit their power for the greater good. In light of this, it could read as, "Blessed are those who have every instinct, every impulse, every passion under control. Blessed are those who are entirely self-controlled."

Many people mistake meekness for weakness, but meekness is, in many ways, the opposite of weakness because it shows strength and self-control that not everybody possesses. Jesus instructs us to be this way as Christians. There are many benefits and rewards in being this way. He tells us one of them in the next phrase; He says, "For they shall inherit the earth," also translated as "They will receive what God has promised." If you can restrain and humble yourself when others cannot, then you've got a reward coming.

In our text, we see this principle at work. Jacob, the patriarch, is about to die, but he lays his hands on all of his sons' heads to speak blessing over their lives before he dies. When he comes to bless his son Joseph, he speaks to him in the third person and says, "Joseph is a fruitful bough even a fruitful bough by a well; whose branches run over the wall. The archers have sorely grieved him, and shot at him, and hated him: But his bow abode in strength and the arms of his hands were made strong by the hands of the mighty God of Jacob."

The truth is that Joseph was indeed a fruitful and successful man, he rose to become the prime minister of Egypt, and in the entire Bible, there isn't a negative thing said about him. Although he was fruitful, his fruitfulness came at a price. As Jacob blesses him, he says, "The archers have sorely grieved him and shot at him and hated him." What did he mean? Because Joseph would rise from the ashes to be successful, it also made him a big target. The archers shot at him; they constantly picked on him; they were always out to get him. He was a target indeed.

They say archery is a coward's way of attacking a person; done from a distance, without close contact; it is not 'person to person' combat. It is like waiting for when a person's back is turned, then taking out your bow and arrow and firing from a distance. That is how it was for Joseph; the devil tried to stop his success by having people shoot at him, and if the enemy used that tactic with Joseph, he could use it with you too.

When the Bible says that "we wrestle not against flesh and blood but principalities, powers, rulers of the darkness of this world, spiritual wickedness in high places," it says our fight is ultimately against the devil but the devil knows how to use people too. I want us to examine the types of shots fired at Joseph that would cause his father to say, "The archers have shot at you."

The arrow of envy

Firstly, we see the 'shot of envy' by his brothers. His brothers envied him so much just because he had received a big dream from God. Some people cannot handle you having a bigger dream, goal or vision than they have. They are ok with you thinking small and believing small, but the idea of you having a dream that enlarges your territory horrifies them much. This was the case with Joseph's elder brothers. "How dare he talk about the moon and the stars bowing down to him." The Bible says; when he told them the dream, they hated him yet the more.

It shows us their hatred for him started even before his dreams. Perhaps the envy was born out of the special attention that his father lavished on him. His father gave him a fancy designer coat whilst they had to make do with their old skins. "Who made you daddy's favourite? They thought, we're just as good as you." You can imagine their questions and hostile remarks. They shot at him and wanted to get rid of him. They ganged up against him, threw him into a pit and left him there to die.

After some time, they saw some slave traders passing, and after giving it much thought, they proceeded to sell Joseph to those traders, deciding that it was an excellent way to get rid of him without actually killing him. These slave traders took him down to Egypt and sold him once again. This time he was sold to a man called Potiphar, a wealthy pollical leader in Egypt. It would prove to be through this association that Joseph would experience the arrow of fury.

The arrow of fury

Joseph became a slave for Potiphar, and because of favour, that seems to be evident in joseph's life, wherever he went and whatever he did seem to bring him popularity, even with Potiphar's wife.

The MSG Bible describes Joseph as being strikingly handsome. Perhaps it was this that made Potiphar's wife so attracted to him. Day after day, she'd approach him and say, "Come to bed with me." History says that Potiphar' wife was a real beauty; she wasn't "mutton dressed up as lamb." She knew how to dress and how to tempt a man. But nothing she did or said was enough to cause Joseph to lower his guard. His repeated reply to her repeated request was, "Ilow can I do this great wickedness and sin against my God." One particular day when Potiphar was out for the day, she grabbed at him and begged him once again to sleep with her.

Joseph wrestles his way out of her grip, causing his coat to come off; that day, Joseph ran for his life, leaving his coat behind.

That famous phrase, "Hell has no fury like a woman scorned," was about to be proven to be true. Because her pride was wounded, as soon as her husband returned, she cried crocodile tears and said to him, "That slave Joseph tried to rape me." When Potiphar heard this, he had Joseph thrown in prison for ten years.

Ancient prisons were not comfortable TV watching prisons that exist today. They didn't afford you the luxuries and freedom that prisoners enjoy nowadays but imagine for a moment, if you can, being stripped of your liberty and choices, deprived of the ability to experience new opportunities and visit new places at will. Imagine having to be confined to a prison cell with very few hours of opportunity to see the outside, and when you do, it is to carry out the laborious task of carrying weight or digging soil. This was the shot of fury sent by Potiphar's wife. Joseph suffered this all for doing what was right.

This, in a strange way, reminds me of that great man Nelson Mandela, who they imprisoned for doing no wrong. He, too, suffered horrors of having to be shut in and told what to do and when to do it. For twenty-seven years, they locked him away like a common criminal, but like Joseph, he wasn't a criminal; he was standing up for justice at a time when seemingly "Black Lives" didn't matter. What could cause a person to be treated so hideously vile? Fury. The shot of fury is a horrendous arrow to face.

The arrow of apathy

Thirdly, Joseph had to experience yet other shooting; this time, it would be the arrow of apathy. While in prison, Joseph came in contact with a butler and a baker, both of whom had dreams that couldn't be interpreted. God gave Joseph the interpretation, and when Joseph interpreted the butler's dream, he told him the good news that after three days, he would be released from prison and restored to his position in the palace. He asked the butler to remember him and put in a good word to the authorities regarding him when he was released. Sadly, the butler, after being released, forgot all about Joseph and left him in prison. This was apathy at its worse: just being forgotten and ignored.

As you can see, Joseph experienced the arrow of envy by his brothers, the arrow of fury by Potiphar's wife and the arrow of apathy by the butler, but in all of this, Joseph did not fire back. He could have fired back; he had the power and the opportunity to get every one of them back. This is what his brothers feared.

When you continue to read the story, you will see that God supernaturally turned Joseph's situation around. Later on, God has Joseph promoted to being prime minister of Egypt, and in Gen 50:15, when Jacob died, all the brothers were afraid because they thought Joseph was going to shoot back.

Genesis 50:16 reads like this. "When Joseph's brothers saw that their father was dead," they said, "What if Joseph holds a grudge against us and pays us back for all the wrongs, we did to him?" So, they sent word to Joseph, saying, "Your father left these instructions before he died: 'This is what you are to say to Joseph: I ask you to forgive your brothers the sins and the wrongs they committed treating you so badly.' Now please forgive the sins of the servants of the God of your father."

Fear had overtaken them, it had convinced them that Joseph would shoot back, but he didn't; in fact, when Joseph received that message, he wept. Then his brothers came and threw themselves down before him and said, "We are your slaves," but Joseph said to them, "Don't be afraid, am I in place of God? You intended to harm me, but God intended it for good to accomplish what is now being done, the saving of many lives." Joseph said, "when you shot at me, what you did, you meant for evil, but it was all a part of God's plan," and they were amazed.

I want you to see that Joseph could have gotten his own back on Potiphar because Potiphar knew his wife was lying; Potiphar knew Joseph wasn't that kind of guy to commit rape. The punishment for rape, especially against a prominent person, was instant execution, but Potiphar simply had Joseph thrown into prison because he knew Joseph was not that kind of guy. When Joseph came into power, he could have said, "Go and get Mr Potiphar, I'm going to teach him a lesson," but he didn't, he didn't shoot.

> "The farther behind I leave the past, the closer I am to forging my own character."
>
> ISABELLE EBERHARDT

Then what about the butler? He could have got his own back on the butler; he could have said, "I'll teach you never to forget me again," but once again, he didn't. This is clearly what Jacob meant when he said, "The archers have sorely grieved him, and shot at him, and hated him: But his bow abode in strength."

Joseph, you had the opportunity to fire back, but you didn't. You could have put them in their place, but you didn't. You had the power and the right legally to shoot back at them, but you didn't; your bow abode in strength.

This story shows us that there is indeed a blessing in not shooting back. It brings with it a great success that would otherwise never be achieved. This is what Jesus was telling us in the beatitudes when he said, blessed are the meek, for they shall inherit the earth. Success on the earth is the inheritance of the meek.

As I close this chapter, I want you to see how Joseph realised that those who take shots at you, those who find faults with you, those who seek to come against you, are all pawns used by the devil. The same devil that uses powers, rulers of darkness and wickedness in high places, is the same devil that will use people to shoot at you.

The good news is that the devil cannot do anything against you without God's permission, and when God allows such things, it is always with the viewpoint of developing you. Joseph said, "you meant it for evil, but God had a different plan," He used it for good. When God allows people to come against you, those people become instruments for your growth and development. The Lord allowed those archers to create in Joseph a character, strength and usability he would never have possessed had he not been shot at. He took the shots and did not retaliate. He did not shoot back.

That day, when Jacob laid his hand on Joseph's head and blessed him, he gave us insight into what it is that brings blessings upon our lives. It is having a meek spirit and not firing back. This will be your test as you continue throughout life; when people try to do you wrong and they just might, will you still do what is right? Nelson Mandela exemplified this. After finally being released from twenty-seven years of imprisonment, he wrote, "As I walked out the door toward that gate that would lead to my freedom, I knew if I didn't leave my bitterness and hatred behind, I'd still be in prison." He, too, went on to be a world leader; he became South Africa's Prime Minister. There is a blessing when you are meek and when you allow your bow to abide in strength. You will live to see the better that is ahead.

"Winning doesn't make you a better person,
but being a better person will make you a winner."

THE MINDS JOURNAL

11

Better Obedience

So, Moses took the staff from the Lord's presence, just as he commanded him. He and Aaron gathered the assembly together in front of the rock and Moses said to them, "Listen, you rebels, must we bring you water out of this rock?" Then Moses raised his arm and struck the rock twice with his staff. Water gushed out, and the community and their livestock drank. But the Lord said to Moses and Aaron, "Because you did not trust in me enough to honour me as holy in the sight of the Israelites, you will not bring this community into the land I give them."

(Num. 20:9-12 KJV)

The first five books of the Bible are often attributed to Moses and referred to as the Torah, the Pentateuch and sometimes Moses' Law. It is clear from scripture that Moses is one of the most important and influential figures in the Bible. God used him to author these books, but he is also a character in the narrative. As early as in the book of Exodus, we see God giving an assignment to him to carry out. This assignment would involve leading the children of Israel out of Egypt and into the Promised Land, a task he could only accomplish with the help of the Lord.

After successfully bringing the children of Israel out of Egypt and crossing the Red Sea, he began this undertaking of leading them to the Promised Land. God had planned for this journey to take only a few weeks, but because they doubted God and His ability to protect and carry them through successfully, God made this three-week journey become a forty-year wilderness experience. Later as they arrived at Kadesh in the wilderness of Zin, Miriam, Moses' elder sister, died.

One can only imagine the kind of pain and grief that Moses was experiencing; Miriam had always been such an important person in his life. From his birth, we see how she protected him when Pharaoh issued a mandate that all male children under a certain age must be killed. When his mother placed him in a basket and made him float down the River Nile, Miriam was the one who watched over him until he reached a place of safety. Also, when Pharaoh's daughter found him and took pity on him, Miriam was the one who suggested that a nurse look after him and recommended Moses' mother.

People who have never lost a loved one will never truly empathise with someone who has; this is what makes Moses' story even more tragic. When Miriam died, the pain Moses felt was unbearable. While he was grieving and mourning the loss of his sister, no doubt still in the process of planning the funeral, he discovers that the children of Israel, those who he had been leading, had formed a committee, and they came to him and began complaining. They whined, saying, "Moses, why did you not leave us in Egypt? It would have better if we had died when everybody else died; now that you've brought us here, there is nothing to drink. We trusted you, and now it seems like we are going to die out here in this wilderness." The Bible says that they complained and murmured. They grumbled about everything; you name it; it was on their list. Can you imagine having to deal with a situation like this during a time of grief, while you're still mourning the loss of your love one?

The pain was so deep that Moses decided to go with Aaron into the Tabernacle of Meeting to spend time with God because there are some things that only God can fix. Moses tells God all that is going on and about the immediate complaint of there being no water to drink, and God tells Moses, "Go outside, talk to the rock, and the rock will give you, its water."

To most of us, this would seem like a crazy command because nobody talks to 'rocks,' after all, 'rocks' cannot talk back. Secondly, they don't have any water to give, but God often will tell you to do things that seem crazy to everybody else because God is after your obedience.

There be will times when God instructs you to do something without giving you an explanation and expects you to do it right away. Delayed obedience is not total obedience, and many times when we try to figure out the command before obeying it, all that does is delay what God wants to do. With God, our understanding of his command can wait, but the obedience of his command cannot. You will never understand some commands until you obey them first.

Sometimes we foolishly offer God partial obedience, too, thinking that will appease Him. We pick the orders we wish to follow and ignore the ones we feel are unreasonable. Commands such as reading the Bible gets the nod, but tithing gets the shake of the head. Attending church receives a thumbs up but forgiving somebody that has done us wrong gets a thumbs down. David said in Psalms 100:2 that we are to serve the Lord with gladness, which means God's commands are to obeyed totally and joyfully. God's word tells us clearly that we can't earn salvation; that comes by grace through faith, but we do bring pleasure to our Father when we obey his commands.

Will you do what God tells you to do, even when you don't understand the reason? Up until now, Moses has, but now he is given this specific command, Moses disobeys. He leaves the presence of God, goes outside, and in blatant disobedience, says to the Israelites, "Listen! you Rebels, how long must we bring water out of this rock?" and instead of speaking to the rock as instructed, he hits the rock not once but twice. This was in no way what God told him to do, but still, we see the faithfulness of God because we notice that even though Moses disobeyed, God still allowed water to gush out of the rock so His people could drink.

> "Obedience is not measured by our ability to obey laws and principles. Obedience is measure by our response to God's voice."
>
> BILL JOHNSON

At this point, because of God's faithfulness in blessing the children of Israel with water, it seemed like everything was alright, but it wasn't; God was displeased. God called both Moses and Aaron and told them that neither of them would enter the Promised Land because of their actions. The very place Moses was leading the Israelites was now going to be the place he would never enter.

On the surface, this seems very harsh. It looks like a cruel punishment for somebody who, up until now, had been faithful. One would think, if God pardoned anyone for getting angry with these "Rebels", Moses would be because Moses had given up so much to fulfil the assignment of leading the children of Israel. He had put his life on the line, and he had jeopardised his family to lead these "stiff-necked" people. These people were so bad that even God wanted to kill them at one point. Surely the reason for God's punishment wasn't just because Moses got angry with God's children; how could it be? We have all been guilty of having anger towards somebody at some point. On further reflection, I suggest that there were several other reasons why God issued such a punishment.

Reason number one could be this: Moses is angry with the Israelites constant complaining and decides to go to the tabernacle of Meeting to communicate this to the Lord. While in the presence of God, the glory of God comes down to commune with Moses, and God tells Moses exactly what to do. After having this experience with God, Moses leaves God's presence, gets angry and does not do what God told him to.

> *"A moment of patience in a moment of anger saves you a hundred moments of regret."*
>
> ALI IBN ABI TALIB

Perhaps the question is, how can Moses go into the tabernacle angry, experience the incredible presence of God and then still leave angry enough to ignore what God had said and strike the rock? In other words, how can one be so angry before going into church, have a supernatural experience with God and then leave just as mad as you were before you entered? When you enter and experience the presence of God, surely there ought to be some change in your attitude?

Secondly, God expects our lives to represent his nature and his love. When Moses complains to God about the Israelites complaining, God does not get angry with them; He simply tells Moses what to do, to produce water. But when Moses comes out from the presence of God angry, the Israelites think God himself is angry. Up until this point, the children of Israel could not go to God themselves. God only spoke to them through Moses. He was the only representation they had of God. Moses' anger caused them to think that God was angry when he was not. Thus, Moses misrepresented God.

My friend, our lives are supposed to represent God to the unsaved world. The only God they will see is what they see in us. God expects us to conduct ourselves in a way that represents and pleases Him. God is love; this is what we must show amid a hate-filled world. I believe God is always disappointed when our witness doesn't match who He is.

The third observation has to do with this Hebrew word 'qādash.' God said to Moses, "it's because you did not trust me enough to honour me as holy." This word qādash can be translated as "to hallo." God was saying, "Moses, you did not hallo Me or separate

Me as Holy." In other words, "you didn't separate Me from you when you said, 'Must we.' If water comes out of a rock, it will have nothing to do with you - it is all Me. I am the God of miracles, not you." As you can see, Moses was giving himself credit; our God will not share his glory with another.

My last suggestion is this. Throughout the Bible, God has always used typologies and symbols. A typology is when something in the Old Testament represents something in the New Testament. When Moses came from the tabernacle angry and hit the rock twice, this would displease God because it messed up typology. This rock represented Christ. This rock typified Christ, and Christ was only going to be smitten once for our sins. He was only going to die once on a cross for mankind. Listen to what the apostle Paul told the church in Corinth:

For I do not want you to be ignorant of the fact, brothers and sisters, that our ancestors were all under the cloud and that they all passed through the sea. They were all baptized into Moses in the cloud and in the sea. They all ate the same spiritual food and drank the same spiritual drink; for they drank from the spiritual rock that accompanied them, and that rock was Christ.

(1Cor. 10:1-4 KJV)

Christ coming and dying for the sins of the world is the message of the Gospel. It is the most important story of the Bible. This story is not to be messed with. You cannot add or take away anything from this story. Could it be that Moses messing with typology and the Gospel story was sufficient to cause his banishment from the Promised Land?

The following text shows us the sad reality of disobeying God's commands. When they finally arrived at the entrance of what would be the Promised Land, the Bible says,

> *And Moses went up from the plains of Moab unto*
> *the mountain of Nebo, to the top of Pisgah, that is*
> *over against Jericho. And the LORD shewed him all*
> *the land of Gilead, unto Dan, And all Naphtali, and*
> *the land of Ephraim, and Manasseh, and all the land*
> *of Judah, unto the utmost sea, And the south, and the*
> *plain of the valley of Jericho, the city of palm trees,*
> *unto Zoar. And the LORD said unto him, this is the*
> *land which I sware unto Abraham, unto Isaac, and*
> *unto Jacob, saying, I will give it unto thy seed: I have*
> *caused thee to see it with thine eyes, but thou shalt*
> *not go over thither. So, Moses the servant of the*
> *LORD died there in the land of Moab, according to*
> *the word of the LORD. And he buried him in a valley*
> *in the land of Moab, over against Bethpeor: but no*
> *man knoweth of his sepulchre unto this day.*

(Deut. 34:1-6 KJV)

As you can see the children of Israel finally arrive at the plains of Moab. Moses climbed Mount Nebo, and God showed him all the land He was about to give the Israelites. Moses is allowed to see it but not allowed to enter it because of what took place in Numbers 20. Moses misses out because of his disobedience.   Moses goes down as one of the best leaders of all time but sadly missed out on seeing the Promised Land in person, however, because of the mercies of God, the following verse shows that Moses got to see it in the spirit in the New Testament.

Jesus took Peter, James and John, led them up a high mountain. There Jesus was transfigured before them. His face shone like the sun, and his clothes became as white as light. Just then there appeared before them Moses and Elijah, talking with Jesus.

(Matt. 17:1 KJV)

Some people are like trees, they take forever to grow up.

ANONYMOUS

12

Getting Your Mind Right

When I was a child, I spake as a child,
I understood as a child, I thought as a child: but
when I became a man, I put away childish things.

(1 Cor. 13:11 KJV)

There is an expectation that as a person grows in age, they'll grow in maturity. It is that expectation of maturation that Paul writes about here in 1 Cor. 13. This chapter is the passage of scripture you'll hear at most weddings. It is that poetic passages of love that talks about what love is and what love is not. It tells you how love is kind, patient and how it keeps no record of wrong. It speaks of love as not being rude and not being boastful. It paints the picture of perfect love. In the midst of painting a portrait of love, Paul speaks about growing up. Almost out of nowhere, he confesses, "When I was a child, I spake as a child, I understood as a child, I thought as a child: but when I became a

> *"Growing old is mandatory; growing up is optional."*
>
> CHILI DAVIS

man, I put away childish things" (1 Cor. 13:11 KJV). The question I'm asking is why Paul would see it necessary to interject this topic here?

In this one statement, Paul challenges us to think about where we are in our maturation. He wants us to consider three areas of our lives, our speaking, understanding and thinking. Could it be possible that Paul shows us that the way a person speaks, understands and thinks, determines what they become? And could it mean that it impacts how we love?

Some people make the mistake in thinking that it is the way they look, and so they spend so much time and money trying to improve the way they look, but according to this text, looks are less important than you think.

Many people may not necessarily have the most incredible looks or perfect features; still, they are more successful and happier than others because their thinking, understanding and speaking are on another level. The way you speak, understand and think is far more critical than the way you look. But most people are willing to confront and change the way they look more than their thinking, speaking and understanding.

Paul understood that these three actions of our life have to change, they have to grow, and they have to develop because as a man thinks in his heart, so he is (Prov. 23:7 KJV). Paul, writing to the Church at Corinth, said something similar when he wrote, "I had to feed you with milk, not with solid food because you weren't ready for anything stronger" (1 Cor. 3:2 NLT). It is the expectation that the longer you have walked with God, the more you should have grown up and the more you've trusted in God, the more mature you ought to be.

Paul says that as a child, he spoke, understood and thought as a child; that is expected behaviour when you are a child, nobody expects any different. When you are immature, it's natural to speak immature things, understand immaturely, think immaturely and react to situations like an immature child does. The problem only comes after this conjunction 'but' after this conjunction, there is a difference in age and stage. What this is dealing with is immaturity on the inside, not the outside. The outside is maturing and showing signs of growing in age all the time but inside the person still acts like a child.

These three actions start in the mind. You speak what comes to mind. You understand with your mind, and you think thoughts with your mind. The mind is the most valuable thing you have in your possession. You have to treasure it, protect it, feed it, build it and guard it. Your mind is under siege all the time. It is being attacked left, right and centre by the world and Satan himself.

"The mind is the battle ground on which every moral and spiritual battle is fought."

J. OSWALD SANDERS

The peril of duplicity

A double minded man
is unstable in all his ways.

(James 1:8 KJV)

James tells about the importance of being single-minded. He says it is the double-minded man who is unstable in everything he does and everything he puts his mind to. The term double-minded comes from the Greek word "dipsuchos," and what it really describes is a person with two minds or souls. A person who cannot settle his mind on a particular way or choice of action; changes his mind with whatever way the wind is blowing. He has become a doubting person who is very much like a sea wave, blown and tossed by the wind.

James says that kind of man should not think he will receive anything from the Lord; he is a double-minded man, unstable in all he does, confused in his thoughts, actions and behaviour. He is like a drunken man swaying from side to side who cannot walk in a straight line. He has no clear direction, and he is in conflict with himself. To be successful in any area, we have to possess a focused mind, fixed and determined. What are you focused on?

The replacement principle

The apostle Paul says the following about our thoughts,

*Finally, brethren, whatsoever things are true,
whatsoever things are honest, whatsoever
things are just, whatsoever things are pure,
whatsoever things are lovely, whatsoever things
are of good report; if there be any virtue, and if
there be any praise, think on these things.*

(Phil. 4:8 KJV)

This text shows us the principle of replacement. The easiest way to get rid of negative thoughts is to replace them with good ones. The Bible says, "Do not be overcome by evil, but overcome evil with good" (Rom. 12:21 KJV). To overcome evil with good may mean turning over the television channel to something more edifying or removing yourself from a gossiping crowd. It may mean partnering with better people, people who are strong where you are weak. Jesus said, "If the blind lead the blind, both will fall into a ditch" (Matt. 15:14). Beggars cannot help beggars; any more than lame people can help the lame people. Right associations are critical, and to make these correct associations, you have to recognise the wrong ones.

Acts 3 tells us of a crippled man that had people carry him daily to a temple, not so that he could worship, but so that he could beg. Those people that brought him looked like they were doing him a favour, but they were not. They appeared to be his friends, but they were not. All they were doing was enabling his disfunction. They were helping him to remain in his current crippled state. You've got to get away from people who help you to be a cripple and get around people who demand better. They are the ones that will help you get up.

Please don't make the mistake of believing just because people are willing to carry you to a gate every day that they are somehow helping you to better your life because, in reality, they are not. All they are doing is enabling your disfunction. Replace them with people who will pull you up. You will be surprised how the Holy Spirit will put strength in your ankles when the right person pulls you. All the people who help you to think negatively, those who encourage you to stay down, you need to move away from and replace them with those who challenge you to get up. Who is it that is around you, speaking into your mind? Spiritually speaking, your mind is one of your most vulnerable organs, and it has to be protected. Moving away from anything and anyone who is negatively influencing your mind is essential.

Over and over again, we are commanded to think right, understand right and speak right. These three areas of life are crucial because they form a system. When you get the system right, everything else is correct, but the problem is that some people want to hold on to a system even though it is not working. Paul said after he became a man, he still had a childish system that he had to put away. It wasn't that he put away childish things, and it made him a man, no! As he became a man and as he grew, he made the decision to put away his childish system. That system may have been acceptable when he was a child, but that system doesn't work for an adult. He had now outgrown how he used to think, speak, and understand, so he put it away.

Now, this "putting away" suggests that I still know where it is, but I cannot use it anymore; it doesn't work for me anymore. This system has to be put away because if you don't put it away, it will put you away. It will put away opportunities, it will put away promotions, it will put away relationships, and it will destroy your better future. Your speaking, understanding and thinking have the power to excel you or demote you.

The power of life and death is in the tongue (Prov.18: 21). God wants you to change the way you speak. And if there be any praise, think on these things. (Phil. 4:8) God wants you to change the way you think. In all thy getting, get understanding (Prov. 4:7). God wants you to change the way you understand.

Somebody once said that understanding is the truth you stand under. In other words, it is your version of what happened and your interpretation of what needs to be fixed. Only when you have a proper understanding of a situation will you be able to look at it objectively.

Not too long ago, a lady visited my church, and after I preached the morning message and closed the service, she approached me and asked permission to speak to me. It became evident that what she wanted to talk about could not be covered in five minutes, so I made an appointment for her to call me. She called, and as she began to speak, I realised her issue was deep. The only way I would ever be able to help was by asking some uncomfortable probing questions. How can you help anyone if you do not truly understand what the problem is? I felt a little awkward asking specific questions, but I knew I couldn't help without full clarification.

Sometimes this is all counsellors do. They know the only way they can genuinely help a person is to understand them and help them understand themself. They are paid money to sit, listen and help you understand your situation. As you begin to speak and unload, they help you to see what needs to be done.

What I am saying is that as long as an heir is underage, he is no different from a slave, although he owns the whole estate. The heir is subject to guardians and trustees until the time set by his father.

(Gal. 4:1-2 NIV)

When talking about the power the Law had before Grace came, Paul says that as long as an heir is underage, he is no different from a slave. He is practically the same as a servant and has the same privileges as a servant even though he owns everything. Even though he owns the whole estate, he is not mature enough to handle what rightfully belongs to him because he is a child who speaks, understands and thinks like a child. He would lose it all, like the prodigal son, if it were given to him at this point. He cannot operate in his lordship because of the way he understands and thinks, and so he is living like a slave even though he is lord of all.

He is subject to guardians and trustees until the time set by his father because of his immaturity. He is under the people he should be over, but because he has not developed and matured to the age and stage where he can handle what is his, he has to wait for the time set by his father, a time when his understanding would be mature enough to handle its true value. Growing older is inevitable but growing up is not. Most of us know somebody in life who grew older but never really grew up. They grew in age but not in maturity. When we grow, here comes the all-important decision, will you put away childish things?

The way we put away these actions is to resist them every time they try to rear themselves. When that temptation calls your phone number, don't answer it. When ugly tries to lure you, don't sink to its level. That childish way of speaking, understanding, and thinking will always try to come to the forefront and be the choice behaviour when you are faced with challenging situations, but just like you do with the devil, resist it, and it will flee. The more you fight thinking that way, understanding that way, speaking that way and reacting that way, the more it will flee. All of these actions start in your mind, and this changed mind will make the difference.

As mentioned before, it was a change of mind that caused the prodigal son to returned home. Once he grew in his mind, once he elevated his mind to another way of thinking, he was able to make the mature decision to return home to the father. When his mind changed, he was put back in his rightful position and his proper relationship. Before, when he had his childish mind, he was not ready for the riches and the entitlement that was supposed to be his, that's why he left and squandered it all, but when he matured, he saw things the right way.

How do you see your future? How do you see success? Do you see it from the perspective of a child that once you attain it, all you're going to do is flaunt it? Are you envisaging spending it as quick as you can and being selfish with it? Or, are you seeing from a mature perspective knowing the responsible thing to do? Jesus told his disciples in John 16:12, "I still have many things to say to you, but you cannot bear them now." However, when the Spirit of truth comes, He will guide you into all truth. He will not speak on His own, but He will speak what He hears, and He will declare to you what is to come."

This verse once again exemplifies the point. It speaks about timing and maturity. If you were to be exposed to too much too fast, then what should be a good thing could actually cause harm. But when the timing is right, and the Holy Spirit reveals to you secrets for your better life, you will be ready to move into position at the right time under the guidance of the Holy Spirit. So, let's make the decision to grow, let's strive for maturity so that when better comes, we will be able to meet it with a better mindset.

As I close this chapter, I want you to consider once again the crippled man lying daily at the gate of the temple. When the time was right, he experienced his miracle, and his life was better. Never again would he need his begging mat or his cup for handouts. Never again would he need to be carried. My friend, whatever your disability, whatever your issue, God wants to raise you up. As your mind is being renewed right now, your ankles are receiving strength. You can get up now. It is time to experience better.

13

Grabbed for Better

Lot was dragging his feet. The men grabbed Lot's arm, and the arms of his wife and daughters God was so merciful to them! dragged them to safety outside the city. When they had them outside, Lot was told, "Now run for your life! Don't look back! Don't stop anywhere on the plain, run for the hills or you'll be swept away."

(Gen 19:16–17 KJV)

The story of Abraham and Lot encompasses many things. It is filled with examples of what and what not to do as we journey towards success in life. So, it would be remiss if we failed to recognise and glean the snippets of instructions weaved within this text's fabric. Like many of the stories in the Bible, Abraham and Lot's story is both gripping and revelatory. It reveals how God can call anyone to accomplish great things. It also illustrates the dangers of making decisions based on external appearances.

The narrative begins in Genesis 12, where we see one of the marvellous promises of success given to anyone in the Bible. Abraham received a calling from the Lord, and with this calling came a great promise of success. God tells Abraham to leave his country, his kindred and father's house and go to a land that God himself would show him. The promise was, if you do this: "I will make of you a great nation, I will bless you and make your name great, you will be a blessing, I will bless those who bless you, and I will curse those who dishonour you, and in you, shall all the families of the earth be blessed" (Gen. 12:1-3).

> *"The life of faith is not a life of mounting up with wings, but a life of walking and not fainting. Faith never knows where it is being led, but it loves and knows the one who is leading."*
>
> OSWALD CHAMBERS

Wow! What a promise. This promise of success included land, a nation, a people, and so much more. Abraham obeys the Lord and takes Sarah, his wife with him, along with their servants and possessions, and the Bible says his nephew Lot also went with him.

Notice, this instruction and promise of success was first given to Abraham. He was the one that was told to leave. He was the one that was promised success and greatness, but the text says Lot went with him. Perhaps the first lesson worthy of gleaning here is the wisdom of staying close to great people.

It wasn't long before they started to see blessings in their lives. Before long, the livestock of Abraham and Lot grew. They grew to such a large degree that there wasn't enough room for both of their livestock and servants to remain in the same place. Arguments started to break out between Abraham's servants and Lot's servants. This illustrates the words of the promise given in Micah 3:10, "I will open the windows of heaven for you. I will pour out a blessing so great you won't have enough room to take it in. Try it! Put me to the test!" (NLT). Only God can give you such a blessing.

Something had to be done; they had outgrown the place, so Abraham and Lot agreed to part ways. Abraham gives Lot the first choice of land.

> *Abraham said to Lot, "Let's not have fighting*
> *between us, between your shepherds and my*
> *shepherds. After all, we're family. Look around. Isn't*
> *there plenty of land out there? Let's separate. If you*
> *go left, I'll go right; if you go right, I'll go left."*

(Gen 13:8–9 MSG)

Abraham sets such an example for us to follow. He exemplifies what the apostle Paul tells us to do in Romans 12:18 about pursuing peace. He allows Lot to choose first. Lot looked and saw the whole plain of the Jordan spread out and well-watered, stretching all the way to Zoar. Lot set out to the east and settled in the cities of the plain and pitched his tent near Sodom.

Notorious places

It is here where we see the beginning of trouble. Lot's choice was a foolish one. Sodom was not a place for a God-fearing person to be living. The Bible tells us the wickedness of Sodom was very great. The people of Sodom were evil, flagrant sinners against God. The grass may have looked attractive, it may have appeared to be green, but greener is not always better.

Little did Lot know that Sodom was known for its sexual immorality. Most people in our generation are now aware of that. Both Christians and non-believers have heard its name mentioned from time to time, and many preachers use it as a launching pad to talk about sexual immorality. This is not surprising as almost every kind of sexual immorality was being practised there. Homosexuality, incest and all kind of sexual deviances, along with blatant disobedience, were seen there. Out of all the places that Lot could have chosen, he chooses this place. This is an example for all of us - never make a big move without prayer. Solomon's words of instruction in proverbs 3:6 attest to this, "In all thy ways acknowledge him, and he shall direct thy paths." It is yet another lesson we must take from this story.

"People do not realize how important decisions are until they make the wrong ones."

Lot chooses to make this place his home, and he lives there with his family, trying not to be contaminated with the prevalent sinful lifestyle. Over time, the behaviour of that city grew worse. It became so despicable in God's eyes that God dispatches angels, not to cleanse the city but to destroy it completely.

It is here that we must pick up on the gravity of the behaviour. When the angels arrive at the city's gates, Lot goes out to greet them. Knowing what the city is like, he invites the visitors to stay at his house. He says, "I don't want you guys to have to rent a room, or a B & B, and this is not the kind of city where you can be out on your own for too long, so come stay with me." The angels go to Lot's house, and not long after arriving, men from all over the city come, and they start banging on Lot's door because the news had got around that some visitors had come into the city and they were staying at Lot's house.

These men outside Lot's house start shouting, "Let the visitors come out so we can have our way with them." They were ready to abuse them sexually. This was the way they wanted to welcome city guests. Lot begins to tell them, listen, these visitors are not the kind of men you want to mess with, so leave them alone. It gets to the point where Lot starts offering his daughters to protect the angels from the callousness of these men, but they are so hell-bent on fulfilling their corrupt sexual desire that they refuse Lot's offer of his daughters and won't take no for an answer.

"You are free to choose, but you are not free from the consequence of your choice."

When the angels see that Lot cannot dissuade these men, they grab and drag Lot back inside the house and with one move of the hand, they strike all the men who were trying to break in, with blindness, leaving them groping in the dark. The angels ask Lot, "Do you have any other family members here in the city? You better get them out of here! Because we're going to destroy this place."

When morning dawned, the angels urged Lot, saying, "Get up, take your wife and your two daughters and whoever else is here. If they don't leave with you, they will be consumed in the impending punishment. Please hurry up; there is no time to play around;

we've got to go." The angels are in haste, but Genesis 19:16 says, "Lot was dragging his feet." How can you be dragging your feet at such a time as this? Can't you see the danger in lollygagging around? The angels grabbed Lot's arm and the arms of his wife and daughters - God being so merciful to them and dragged them to safety outside the city.

Thank God for the grabbing

Some of us are in the right place today, simply because grace grabbed us. You didn't want to leave the streets because the streets were all you knew, but it was killing you slowly, and so God's grace had to grab you. Somebody else didn't want to leave the comfort of that person's bed because it felt so good to the flesh, but it was destroying your future, so God's grace had to grab you.

"Grace changes everything."

And yet there's another person who didn't want to leave that job because it was comfortable, although mind-numbing and taking you nowhere fast, and so grace had to grab you. And here is the thing about being grabbed, it is never comfortable. It feels wrenching, and it hurts, but it produces movement and growth. It was this I alluded to earlier. When God grabbed me from the musical world, He grabbed me to fulfil a purpose. When he grabbed me, others left what they were doing and started following. It was a domino effect. Their purpose came in view too. Because I was following my purpose, they also began to walk in theirs.

What is clear from this text is that sometimes we fail to see the seriousness of our delay. God is a God of timing, he has an appointed time for everything, and when we delay, we run the risk of missing out on what God has for us. The text says that the angels had to grab Lot and his family to force them to safety. It wasn't God's will for them to die in Sodom's destruction, God had a better future in mind for them, but as you can see, they had to be manhandled or, should I say, grabbed to experience it.

Once outside of the city, the angels told Lot and his family, "Run for your life! Don't look back! Don't stop anywhere on the plain. Run for the hills, or you'll be swept away." Despite the angels giving them specific instructions of where to go, the Bible says Lot protested. He replied, "I know that you've shown me an immense favour in saving my life, but I can't run for the mountains; who knows what terrible thing might happen to me in the mountains. But look over there, that town is close enough to get to. It's a small town, hardly anything to it. Let me escape there and save my life" (Gen. 19:18-20 KJV).

> "Obedience is your responsibility.
> The outcome is God's."
>
> STEVEN FURTICK

Once again, Lot is procrastinating and disobeying. God wants him to go up to the mountain. Up is a better location; up signifies growth and gives you a better vantage point, but he wants to go over to a little town called Zoar.

Can you imagine what the angels are thinking? Firstly, we tell you to move quickly; and you don't - you linger, so we have to drag you out of the city; then we give you an instruction to go to the hills because that's the best place for you and you won't obey us on that either. You're telling us what is best for you, even though we have been sent from the omniscient One. You failed to see that God wants you to go up to the hills where He has high plans and high hopes for you. It is a high place where you will have impact and influence, but you would rather go to a little place where you'll have no influence and remain ordinary because of your myopia.

God has something much better waiting for him, but he thinks so little of himself, he would instead go to a little place. There are so many things in life that God has placed before us and planned for us, but because we erroneously believe that we know better than God, we tell him, "Let me do it this way." Listen! If God tells you to go somewhere, please understand that He wants to bring better your way. After Lot pleaded, God in his permissive will said to him, "sure! I will still send favour with you." Our God is that kind of God. He allows us to have free will and yet sends a grace that will follow.

Better is ahead not behind

One of the saddest parts of this story is the reality that sometimes not everybody will enjoy the success we have. The better life that God wants us to experience and enjoy in this life requires following instructions. Like many of the promises in the Bible, many of them are conditional. If you do this – then I God will do that. With the permission granted to go to Zoar, the angels gave Lot and his family a final command, and with this one, there could be no compromise. He tells them, "When on your way to the city, whatever you do, and whatever you hear - don't look back."

As Lot began to run, with his daughters close behind him, his wife lagged behind, and from that position, when she heard the sound of destruction, she looked back. She turned and watched the flaming sulphur fall from the sky, consuming everything she valued, and she sadly looked back. We don't know if her death was a punishment for loving her old life so much that she failed to obey God's command, or if it was a consequence of her reluctance to leave her old life quickly, but her disobedience brought an end to her life, she turned into a pillar of salt.

God had such a great future for her. A better life was ahead, their names would have been famous for accomplishments, but instead, she is used as an example of what not to do. Jesus later says in Luke 17:32, when warning his followers – "Remember Lot's wife".

"*No matter where we are in life, God has more in store.*
He never wants us to quit growing."

ANONYMOUS

14

More Than Better

*When all the jugs and bowls were full, she said to one
of her sons, "Another jug, please." He said, "That's it.
There are no more jugs." Then the oil stopped.*

(2 Kings 4:6 MSG)

I once heard a story about a lady who always made a beautiful ham for the holidays. Before she placed the ham in the oven to cook, she would always cut off a piece at each end. One day her young daughter was watching and asked, "Mum, why do you always cut off the ends of the ham?" The mother replied, "This is how my mother always did it," so in reality, she was just cooking her ham the way her mother had taught her. After the girl's mom thought about it for a while, she decided to call her own mother to ask why the ends of the ham needed to be cut off? The response on the other end of the phone was a chuckle, followed by, "I used to cut the ham ends off because my pan was too small to hold all of it."

It's a comical story, but metaphorically, the question we must ask is, how many of us have been cutting off ends rather than getting larger pans and larger vision for our lives? We've become comfortable and complacent with the way things have always been that we don't think to question old traditions. We see and hear things and accept them as our reality, but think for a moment, what would happen if we just got a bigger pot? What more would we be able to do and receive if we enlarged our capacity?

The more I read the Word and grow in God, is the more I see that there are no limits to what God can do in a person's life. It has become so glaringly obvious that we are the ones who put limits on ourselves. We tell ourselves that this is all we can expect to be. This is how far we can expect to go. This is how much we can expect to earn, and this is how much we should expect to achieve. Those expectations become limitations that we put on ourselves - if we could only understand that we need to break out of those boxes.

Solomon warns us in Proverb 23:7 "For as he thinks in his heart, so is he." God wants to stretch us way beyond what we've always thought was our limit, but to do that, he has got to get us thinking differently. It has been said, "If you can change your thinking, you will change your mindset. If you change your mindset, you will see your destiny." Don't ever allow your friends, culture, race, or environment to dictate what you can do or how far you can go. Where you are right now is probably the subtotal of your thoughts thus far. But there are absolutely no boundaries to what you can do and become in life. This understanding is crucial as we pursue success in achieving better.

I tried to get this message across to a friend of mine as we went out to dinner after attending a Pastors' Conference in Orlando, Florida. While seated around the table, I couldn't help noticing that the waitress taking our order was Spanish, so I ordered my meal in Spanish. It seemed to be such a amazing thing in the eyes of both my friend and the waitress, but what they didn't know is that a few years before that, I made the decision that I would teach myself Spanish. Why? To prove to myself that I could be multilingual if I tried. I told my colleague, with just the right mindset and a commitment to it, you too could learn that language; it is well within your grasp. Immediately after saying that, he replied, "No, my brain can't take that." I looked at him glaringly and said, "who told you that lie?" Limits are lies dressed up in reason.

One of my all-time favourite verses in the Bible is Paul's admission to the Corinthian church; he said, "I can do all things through Christ who strengthens me." That used to be my go-to-verse, growing up as a child, and now it has become the motto by which I live. When we live that way, we take the limits off. All things do not mean some things; all things mean all things, even the things that life says are impossible. Peter experienced this first hand.

> And Peter answered Him and said, "Lord, if it is You, command me to come to You on the water." So, He said, "Come." And when Peter had come down out of the boat, he walked on the water to go to Jesus.

(Mt 14:28–29 NKJ)

Jesus stood out in the water, looked at Peter, and said, "you can do this." He wanted Peter to take a step of faith, knowing all the others in the boat would not. Jesus wanted Peter to trust him and to believe that there are no limits to what he could do, with Jesus by his side. But most of the time, we are afraid to step out and enlarge our territory for fear of falling, but falling is not failing. The Bible says, "For a righteous man may fall seven times and rise again" (Pr. 24:16 KJV). Falling simply teaches us how to do it better the next time. Peter may have fallen the first time, but he was helped up and never fell in that way again; in fact, both Peter and Jesus continued to walk on water. Don't you see what Jesus is telling us? There are great things for you to do. Jesus, in trying to teach this lesson, further spoke these words:

> *"Always remember, you have within you the strength, the patience and the passion to reach for the stars to change the world."*
>
> HARRIET TUBMAN

> *"Very truly I tell you, whoever believes in me will do the works I have been doing, and they will do even greater things than these, because I am going to the Father"*

(Jn 14:12 NIV)

I find this scripture both fascinating and challenging. After raising the dead, casting out evil spirits, restoring the sight of the blind and unblocking deaf ears, Jesus tells us that we are to do greater things than these. Isn't it crazy how our thoughts are of limiting ourselves, whilst Jesus wants to remove all the limits that we put up? Even the very things God wants to give us, we inadvertently talk ourselves out of receiving them. Do you know that Jesus has given us a blank cheque? Sounds crazy, right? But listen to what he tells us in Matthew 7:7:

Ask, and it will be given to you; seek, and you will find; knock, and it will be opened to you. For everyone who asks receives, and he who seeks finds, and to him who knocks it will be opened. Or what man is there among you who, if his son asks for bread, will give him a stone? Or if he asks for a fish, will he give him a serpent? If you then, being evil, know how to give good gifts to your children, how much more will your Father who is in heaven give good things to those who ask Him!

(Matt. 7:7 NKJV)

I love the directness of the Message Bible. It renders it this way

Don't bargain with God. Be direct. Ask for what you need. This isn't a cat-and-mouse, hide-and-seek game we're in. If your child asks for bread, do you trick him with sawdust? If he asks for fish, do you scare him with a live snake on his plate? As bad as you are, you wouldn't think of such a thing. You're at least decent to your own children. So, don't you think the God who conceived you in love will be even better?

(Matt. 7:7 MSG)

So, this lets us know that we can dare to think and dream big. If Jesus says we can ask for whatever we want, that we don't have to

159

be timid or indecisive, we don't have to be hesitant; then we can take the limits off and be bold in our request. The size of the blessings we can contain is limited only to the extent of our capacity to receive. God has more than enough to give, but do you have the capacity mindset to receive. The story of 2 kings 4 poignantly explains this.

The context is simply this: This woman's husband passed away, leaving her with no income stream. He was a God-fearing man, but now that he had died and was in debt, the creditors were on their way to the woman's house to collect on the debt. They were going to take her children to be slaves as payment for the debt. When she saw Elisha, she cried out to him, telling him the whole story. Her situation was dire, to say the least. When Elisha, the man of God heard, he asked, "Tell me, what do you have in your house?" She said, "all I have is a little oil." Elisha said, "Here's what you do, go up and down the street and borrow jugs and bowls from all your neighbours. Get as many as you can. Then come home, you and your sons and lock the door behind you, pour oil into each container; when each is full, put it aside."

This was a strange command, but she did exactly as she was told in desperation and obedience. And as she began to pour oil from her little bottle into the first jug, the oil miraculous continue to flow until the jug was full. She then began to pour it into the second jug, and that too became full. She then poured oil into the third jug, and miraculously it became full also. She kept requesting more containers from her sons to fill them up. After many times of asking, her sons said, Mum, there are no more, and the Bible says, then the oil stopped flowing. She was able to sell the oil to pay off all off her debts and had much more leftover on which she could live. Do you see how our God is a God of more than enough?

What a miracle, as long as she had the capacity to hold more, she got more. God can only pour into us what we have the capacity to receive. This is what we need to be cognizant of. When Elisha met this woman, he basically said, "what is it that you need? I'm a man of God. What do you want God to do for you?" And once she told him, he made it happen. Her blessing was huge, limited only by her capacity to receive. Do you see how it works? Enlarge the capacity of your faith and enlarge your blessing.

Jabez asked for and did the same. He prayed for a blessing and enlargement in 1 Ch 4:10. And Jabez called on the God of Israel saying, "Oh, that You would bless me indeed, and enlarge my territory, that Your hand would be with me, and that You would keep me from evil, that I may not cause pain!" So, God granted him what he requested.

I am totally convinced that if we would only enlarge our capacity to receive more, and if we would enlarge our faith, we would receive the miraculous.

Now all glory to God, who is able, through his
mighty power at work within us, to accomplish
infinitely more than we might ask or think.

(Eph. 3:20 NLT)

God wants to work with us, and in us; It's a partnership. Allowing His mighty power to be at work within us is our part.

161

Accomplishing is His part. The word 'accomplish' signifies that something actually gets done. This isn't a 'maybe it will happen,' this is a for sure it will happen, and how much can He accomplish? It's infinite. It's more than we can ever ask or think. What He is able to accomplish through us when we yield to His power is simply mind-blowing. So, we have to develop a "No more limits mindset" to receive the 'Better' that is ahead.

"You must learn a new way to think,
before you can master a new way to be."

MIRIANNE WILLIAMSON

15

Eliminating Stinking Thinking

And Jacob their father said unto them, Me have
ye bereaved of my children: Joseph is not, and
Simeon is not, and ye will take Benjamin away:
all these things are against me.

(Gen. 42:36 KJV)

Everybody that is reading this book today has been blessed more than they know. Being alive with all your faculties intact is one of the greatest blessings one can receive. Contrary to what you may believe, not everybody made it over to see this New Year that you are currently seeing. As I get older, the number of funerals I attend seems to increase with the years. I went to many of them last year all over the country, some of them were for young people, others for the old, some were friends, others for family, some died from sickness, others from murder and sadly some even took their own lives. I am now noticing as the years roll on, I seem to know more people who are currently in heaven than friends who are still on earth, so when I tell you, "You're blessed to see another year," please believe that what I am telling you is correct. And I don't think that God spared your life to see a New Year for you to just have another 365 days of the same kind of mundane life. Your life was spared for a reason. God has great things in store.

But with this comes good news and bad news. The bad news is, I wish I could tell you that throughout the rest of this year, you won't have any problems. I wish I could guarantee that you won't have any financial issues, relational issues, health issues, family issues or problems on the job. If I told you that, I wouldn't be telling you the absolute truth because we are now living in the last days.

> "Problems are not stop signs, they are guidelines."
>
> ROBERT H SCHULLER

The Bible says in 2 Timothy 3:1, that in the last days perilous times will come, and then it gives us a description of how people will act and how they will be, and it is not a pretty picture. It goes on to describe them as being "lovers of themselves, lovers of money, boastful, arrogant, abusive, disobedient to their parents, ungrateful, unholy, unloving, unforgiving, slanderous, without self-control, brutal, without the love of God."

With such a description of the things in the last days, it is evident that problems will increase, but to the believer, problems do not serve as stop signs but guidelines. Every year we see the above on a grander scale, and on top of all this, the Bible also reminds us, "They that live godly must suffer persecution." Anytime you decide to live for God, the enemy turns up the heat. You don't have to go looking for trouble; trouble knows where you live.

At the time of writing this chapter, my mother is battling dementia, my father is battling the effects of a stroke that has left him with the challenge of being able to walk like he once did. My brother-in-law is lying unconscious in a hospital bed from a stroke, and I am recovering from a shoulder surgery that doesn't seem to want to heal. All of this, and it is only the beginning of the year, but here is the good news, as Christians, when trouble shows its face, we have a choice as to how we respond. We can either

> *"Change your character and your character will change you."*

face situations with a positive spiritual mindset or face them with a negative carnal mindset. We can either face them with: "Many are the afflictions of the righteous, but the Lord delivers them out of them all" attitude, or we can face them with an attitude that says, "Woe is me – this thing is going to kill me." How we face challenges is critical. The Bible says, "As a man thinks, so is he."

In this text, God had already changed Jacob's name. The name Jacob meant supplanter, trickster or fraudster, but God had plans for Jacob. He was going to use him mightily, in a way that nobody had been used before, but his name Jacob would have been a great hindrance to his destiny. It's so important that we be mindful of the names we give our children; I know certain names sound good, but what do they mean?

I grew up disliking my name because children can be mean, and so often, I would be subjected to listening to that old nursery rhyme

- Simple Simon met a pie-man going to a fair. Others, when they saw me, would play the game – Simon Says. Although some would say that wasn't anything to be upset about, hearing this year in and year out took its toll. After a while, I was willing to fight anybody that would dare to recite it. But then I found out what my name meant, it changed my outlook on life totally. It means "Heard by the Lord." When I discovered that, I started to appreciate it. When you call me, you are actually declaring that the Lord hears me.

When they called Jacob's name, they were declaring him to be a trickster, supplanter and fraudster, but God wanted to use him but couldn't use him like that, and so God changes his name from Jacob to Israel (Governed by God).

This Jacob who was now named Israel was the Father of Joseph, Benjamin and ten other sons who collectively later would become the twelve tribes of Israel. But notice in our text, he is not being called by Israel - his new name, he is being called by Jacob his old name. Why? Why would God change his name and then refer to him by his old name? Part of the reason is that here in the text, he is acting "Jacoby" again. Trouble has come his way, and instead of facing trouble with his new name - Governed by God, He has reverted to his old mentality, his old way of thinking, he is frustrated and fearful, and cries out because he is in turmoil, "All these things are working against me."

Have you ever felt like that? Have you ever been in a situation where everything seems to be against you? He utters these words because he can't see the full picture, and none of us can. The apostle tells us in 1 Cor. 13:12, "We see through a glass darkly." We don't see things as clearly as we think we do, and because we can't see clearly, it causes frustration to rise when negative things come our way. But you and I are still a lot better than Jacob because when trouble comes our way as Christians, we have the promise of Romans 8:28, "For we know that all things work together for good to them that love the Lord." Jacob didn't have that verse memorized, and because Jacob doesn't know better, he says in the text "All these things are against me."

The problem

Why would he say that? What had gone wrong? Well, put yourself in his shoes. The Bible says there was a terrible famine in the land. At this point, they had gone without food for weeks. Can you imagine the pain of being without food for weeks? We feel miserable going without food for a day; that's why some struggle to fast. Most of us eat not only out of necessity but also for pleasure, but with famine, there is no food whatsoever. This famine in Canaan was severe and intense. Jacob knew that before long unless God intervened, they would starve to death. However, reports were coming out of Egypt that they had stored up grain, and they had supplies of food.

Jacob looked at his eleven sons because one of his sons, his favourite son Joseph was dead (or so he thought), and so Jacob said to his boys, "Go down to Egypt and see what you can do, try to buy food, if not we're all going to die." After instructing them, he told them not to take Benjamin with them. Benjamin was his youngest, and his second favourite son. Joseph, his first favourite son, was believed to be already dead, and he was afraid of anything bad happening to Benjamin.

Joseph and Benjamin were full brothers; Jacob had them with his favourite wife, Rachael. Initially, Rachel was barren, but she cried out to God, "Give me children lest I die." And God did give her children and then she did die. He gave her Joseph and then Benjamin, and it was while she was giving birth to Benjamin that she died in labour, and because he loved Rachael so much, he loved the boys that came from their union. His other sons were born to different women, thus making them half-brothers. There wasn't a doubt that he loved his ten eldest sons, but he didn't love them as much as he loved Joseph and Benjamin, so when he told them, "Go down to Egypt without Benjamin" he was dead serious.

Jacob believed Joseph had died at his brothers' hands, perhaps through foul play but couldn't prove it. He thought it because that day when Jacob sent Joseph to check up on his brothers, they grabbed him – took his coat- threw him in a pit, and they were going to leave him to die in the heat, but quickly changed their minds when they saw slave traders approaching. Instead, they sold him to the slave traders that were passing by. Those slave traders sold him to a man named Potiphar for whom he worked many years. Joseph later had to do a ten-year stint in prison, but the Bible tells us, "But the Lord was with him."

Joseph goes through a series of events in his life, and he ends up interpreting the dreams of two of his inmates, which leads to him interpreting the dream of Pharaoh himself. Being grateful, Pharaoh sets him free and promotes him. Jacob ends up being second in command in Egypt because his gift made room for him, but his father Jacob thinks he is dead because when they sold Joseph, they stripped him of his coat, smeared it with animal blood and brought it back to Jacob, their father, supposing that a wild animal had killed Jacob. That day, the Bible says, "Jacob could not be comforted."

Back to our text, Jacob tells his boys to go down to Egypt to get food, but they are forbidden to take Benjamin. So, the sons go down to Egypt, and when they get there, they stand before the man in charge of food distribution. Little do they know that this man is their brother, Joseph, albeit fully grown now and with authority. They don't recognize who he is, but Joseph recognizes them and precedes them to play a game. He looks at them and says, "You guys are spies," to which they reply, "Oh no, sir! We're not spies; we live in Canaan up north. We live with our father and our younger brother Benjamin, but where we've come from, there is a famine and people are dying; we've come with money to buy food."

Joseph replied, "I don't believe you. The only way I'll believe that you're not spies is if you go back home and bring this younger brother Benjamin that you speak about and in the meantime – YOU Simeon - you stay here until they return," and he commands the guards to arrest Simeon. He takes their money and gives them a little food and sends them on their way and at this point Joseph is testing them.

What could they do? Simeon is now held as a hostage. They get home and they say, "Dad, we've got the food," but when they open up the sack, to their horror, they see both the food and the money which had somehow ended up back in the bag, and they are thinking, "Oh no! This is going to look like robbery." On top of that, now they have to tell Jacob the news. "Dad, they kept Simeon, and the man in charge of the distribution of food down there says, the only way we are going to get Simeon back is if we bring Benjamin;"

and Jacob cries out, "No way! Joseph is not, and Simeon is not, and ye will take Benjamin away: all these things are against me."

That is how we can feel when things go wrong, when we lose jobs, when the doctor gives us an evil report, when relationships are threatening to come apart at the seams and when the pressure keeps mounting. We tend to allow our old nature and our old outlook to take over, but if we could only see how God is working behind the scenes. Behind the scenes, things were changing; things were working for good. There was a miracle in play. God would say, "Jacob, you don't know, Joseph is not dead; he is Prime Minister."

"Stay open minded, things aren't always what they seem to be."

For someone reading this book, you too have been waiting years for some things to happen, and you're asking: When will things get better? When will this problem be over? Are things ever going to turn around? When will that solution come? When will I find my significant other? Listen, God is working behind the scenes, and the one thing you can be sure of is that "All things are working together for good to them who love the Lord" (Rom 8:28). Remember, "No good thing will he withhold from those who walk uprightly" (Psalm 84:11). You cannot be a Christian, and things not work out better in some way or the other.

Now let's look at whom the promise is to, notice it says, "to them who love the Lord." Are you someone who can genuinely say, I love the Lord? What does it mean to love the Lord? Peter was asked this question too. After denying Christ three times, when Jesus was ready to reinstate him, He asks Peter the question, Peter, do you love me? Peter replies, yes, Lord, I love you, and Jesus said, then feed my sheep.

Three times this question was asked, and three times Peter affirmed his love for Christ and each time Jesus told Peter what he had to do to prove his love. If you want to prove you love me, take care of my sheep. Take care of my people because my people are an extension of me; I am the head, and they are my body. When I need somebody to go somewhere, I use their feet; when I need somebody to do something, I use their hands; when I need somebody to show love, I use their arms; when I need to speak a word of love, I use their mouths. Jesus is saying, if you really love me, it will be seen in the way you treat my people. It can be seen in the way you love my people. If you love them, you love me.

Jesus expanded on this further when he said in John 14:15, "If you love me, keep my commandments." When you look at the Ten Commandments listed in Exodus 20, the first five deals with our relationship with God, the second five deals with our relationship with each other; Jesus went on to say; this is my commandment that you love one another (John 15:12).

"Taking care of others is called humanity."

Once we begin loving the way God tells us to love, we can rest assured that God will make all things work together for our good no matter what we go through. That's why David said, "Trust in the Lord with all thy heart and lean not to your own understanding" (Prov.3:5).

Throughout the rest of this year, things may come your way that you don't understand, but during this time, you must trust that He is working it for your good. Jacob was wrong; all these things were not working against him but for him. That was nothing but stinking thinking; it is not how believers are supposed to think.

His sons eventually went back to Egypt and brought their younger brother Benjamin with them. As they stood in front of Joseph, the new Prime Minister, Joseph, after testing them further, revealed his identity to his brothers. He said, "I'm Joseph, your brother, the one you sold into slavery. You meant it for evil, but God turned it around for good. God sent me here ahead of time to preserve you, go and get father and all of the brethren, tell them to come and live with us in Egypt." They all left Canaan and went to live in Egypt in a place called Goshen. No more famine; they now had an abundance. Things definitely got better.

This text reveals in a rather subtle way that sometimes we think so incorrectly about situations. Jacob was convinced that nothing was going his way and that everything was working against him. It was so far from the truth. It is the kind of stinking thinking and lies that the devil will always try to feed us. He is a liar from the beginning. Anytime he whispers negatively in your ear and says things like, "You won't make it through this, you'll never be anything, this is going to make you lose your mind, or this sickness is going to kill you;" remember it is the voice of the liar, call that voice what it is - a liar. Don't entertain his voice any longer.

This is important because the predicaments you find yourself in do not define your destiny. Predicaments can lie on the future. That financial predicament, it's only temporary; that health condition does not have to be yours in the future, 'Better is ahead.' You are what God says you are, and you can be what God says you can be.

So, refuse to think the worse, God hasn't planned any defeats for you. Let God's truth anchor your thoughts. Jesus said, "You will know the truth, and the truth will set you free" (John 8:32). Set yourself free in the mind, soul and body. Make your future bright and better, "Better is Ahead."

"*When you are transitioning to a new season of life,
the people and situations that no longer fit you will fall away.*"

MANDY HALE

16

Transitioning to Better

Then Joshua commanded the officers of the people, saying, "Pass through the camp and command the people, saying, 'Prepare provisions for yourselves, for within three days you will cross over this Jordan, to go in to possess the land which the LORD your God is giving you to possess.

(Josh. 1:10-11)

According to the Cambridge Dictionary: Transition is "a period of changing from one state or condition to another; a change from one form or type to another, or the process by which this happens". So, by definition, movement has to take place, change has to occur, and development has to be achieved. This movement, however, is always positive, but just because it is positive doesn't mean it won't cause pain. For a child to transition from the comfort of the womb to the coldness of the world's environment or from the familiar to the unknown causes him and his mother much pain. Still, just because there is pain involved in the transition, it doesn't mean it's not positive, so don't ever try to avoid the process.

Many people have not reached the destiny that God has for them because they have not been able to handle transitions well. Whilst earthly teachers may allow you to pass onto the next grade and stage without finishing all the assignments and completing all the course work needed, God will not. God is the perfect teacher, and he will not let you move onto the next stage or grade before time.

Transition also requires that we have the correct mindset; without the proper perspective, pain and difficulty will make you give up on the process. Real goals take time to achieve. During the process, there may be times where you feel like you've already failed, times where you feel like it is pointless to keep going, and times where you wonder are you even on the right path, but no matter what the setback, trust that you are capable of achieving and have patience.

"The greatest mistake you can make in life is to be continually fearing you will make one."

ELBERT HUBBARD

It is this mindset that Michael Jordan adopted when he wanted to become great. After achieving greatness, he said, "I've missed more than 9000 shots in my career. I've lost almost 300 games. Twenty-six times I've been trusted to take the game-winning shot and missed. I've failed over and over again in my life, and that is why I succeeded." Do you see? Giving up will never reward you with 'Better,' but having the correct mindset will.

When the children of Israel were set free from Egyptian bondage, God had incredible plans for them; not only were they going to be a freed people, but they would dwell in their own land, a land flowing with milk and honey, but for them to transition to this place they would need the right mindset. This would prove to take time because after being slaves for so long without a glimmer of hope of ever being free, it had conditioned their minds to only knowing slavery and bondage. Pharaoh had refused to let them go time and time again, but God used his servant Moses to inflict plagues on Egypt. After inflicting ten plagues, Pharaoh eventually conceded to allowing God's people to go. It would be the beginning of their transition.

Their first challenge came as they approached the Red Sea. While camped at the Red Sea, they heard the sound of chariots in the distance; Pharaoh had changed his mind. When they turned around and saw that Pharaoh's army was pursuing them and that the Red Sea was in front of them, with mountains on both sides, they began to cry out to Moses. "Moses, didn't we tell you to leave us alone in Egypt, but no! You insisted on bringing us out here to the middle of nowhere, and now Pharaoh is right behind us, and we have nowhere to go. Moses, you've messed up."

They saw the Red Sea as a closed-door, but it was just an obstacle that needed to be overcome in reality. Isn't this the same in life? During transition, we come across many obstacles too. God allows obstacles to cross our path, to teach us how to endure. He allows mountains to teach us how to climb and problems, teach us how to pray. God uses obstacles to grow us. Don't ever conclude that they are doors permanently shut just because they seem hard to get around.

To the children of Israel, this seemed to be a door shut with the keys locked away, but to Moses, this was nothing but an obstacle. Moses shouted, "Stand still and see the salvation of the Lord." And when Moses lifted his rod, God supernaturally opened the Red Sea for the children of Israel to cross over. That would prove to be the last day they ever had to deal with Pharaoh and his army. They were finally free.

It wasn't long before they journeyed to a place called Kadesh Barnea (Num14:40). From there, they sent twelve spies to check out part of the land that God had promised them. When the spies came back, ten of them came back with a negative report. They reported, "Yes, the land is great, it is all that God said it would be, it flows with milk and honey, and the grapes are so big it takes two men to carry a cluster, but here's the bad news, there are giants in the land, they are huge, and we look like grasshoppers to them, so let's go back to Egypt."

> *"Honor the space between no longer and not yet."*
>
> NANCY LEVIN

Ten of them came back with a negative report, but two of the spies were more believing. They reported, "Yes, it's true that we are little, and they are big, but our God is bigger, and we can take the land." But the children of Israel did not listen to the two spies; instead, they followed the majority. Because of this, God did not allow that generation to go into the promised land; he made them go around the wilderness for forty years until the entire generation had died out. God did not want that mentality to be carried over into the promised land.

During those forty years, Moses died, and God chose Joshua to be the next leader. Joshua took over from Moses, and after that whole generation had died out, we see the beginning of their pilgrimage into the promised land. God was now preparing them to cross over another body of water, which would prove to be another challenge to their transition. These waters were the River Jordan. There are three things we see in the text that is necessary for transition.

Positioning

As we get ready to talk about positioning, we can liken it to the game of chess. Chess is mostly about positioning; if you can arrange for your pieces to be in the right positions, you win the game. This is true for the game of life too. A lot of what you go through in life is about positioning; God is positioning you for your assignment. When God is in charge of your life, whatever you are doing, God is behind the scenes, moving the chess pieces of your life to line up. So that when you get to where he needs you to be, you will already be lined up with the people you need to be lined up with, and you will be around the things you need to be around. He is positioning things.

The preparation process

Everything you've gone through in life is used to prepare you for where God is taking you. Nothing is wasted, no experience is worthless or redundant, God uses everything, and God will navigate you through the necessary experiences to prepare you for the destination ahead.

God will not usher you into the destiny he has ordained for you until you are prepared. He prepares each of us in unique ways, and God often uses multiple streams of preparation; Some of which only makes sense once we have come out on the other end and are privileged to look back. Everybody that was used to accomplish great things in the Bible, went through their time of preparation. Here are just a few:

David was prepared through many streams by having to fulfil ordinary, mundane tasks such as tending and protecting sheep, times of obscurity, musical training, being rejected by his father, being pursued by King Saul, but all of these experiences prepared for him 'Better.'

Moses, being given up at birth, led to his excellent preparation. It caused him to be bilingual and bicultural and, at the same time, a man of great strength. This later gave him empathy for his own people.

Mary being a virgin, would need special preparation for what God would call her to do. So, an angel was dispatched in person to prepare and reassure her. Later she was sent to her cousin Elizabeth's house and was reassured again that she was indeed carrying the Christ when John the Baptise leapt in his mother's womb.

"Success occurs when opportunity meets preparation."

ZIG ZIGLAR

Esther, another godly woman in the Bible, was prepared and guided through her relationship with her uncle. Only after this would she be able to make the bold statement, "If I perish, I perish but I must see the king" (Esther 4:16).

Paul was prepared through the family connections he was born into, the training he received, the positions he held, and when Christ finally saved him on the Damascus Road, it was then through a time of obscurity and teaching. God always prepares us for our assignment.

With God, he is able to use everything we go through in life as preparation. The devil may have meant it for evil, but God turns it around for good. He causes all things to work together for good. I want you to think for a minute about some of your past experiences, good and bad, and although you may not see it now, I can assure you, they become purposeful. I had no idea the tests I had to endure in life would become testimonies, but they have. I now can use them as examples in preaching, teaching and counselling, and I can also look back at them now without them causing me pain.

My friend, as you are being prepared for 'Better,' may you hear God's voice encouraging you, "Fear not, for I have called you. I'll go before you, beside you, and behind you."

The purging process

The process of purging is vital. Purging is defined as to free from impurities, to purify, to remove by cleansing, to get rid of sin, guilt, defilement, and to empty. This process is a part of spiritual growth. Just as your physical body needs to be purged from the toxins that accumulate due to faulty nutrition or a contaminated environment, so your mind and spirit need to undergo a similar cleansing process. It's the part where the things that are not like Christ have to be removed from our lives to produce spiritual maturity.

Whenever your body begins to rid itself of toxins, initially, it is never a pleasant experience. You feel weak and uncomfortable at first as you move through the process, but soon you start experiencing the benefits, like an energetic renewal and an elevated state of being. Some of what we go through in life is God purging stuff out of us that is no good for us. There are some things God has to remove; there are some habits God has to break; there are some attitudes God has to get out.

It is no wonder purging has been likened to the act of vomiting and just like vomiting, which is an involuntary spasmodic movement that causes ejection from the mouth; purging too is an involuntary spasmodic movement that causes ejection from the heart. Most of the time, we are not aware of what needs to be removed from our lives and our thinking, but God does; this is why it is involuntary. God wants to and has to remove anything and everything that does not conform to His Son, and by the time He is finished, we will be ready to step into our promised land.

"Purge, emerge and flourish its natural."

TIM JOHNSON

God is saying, "I cannot take you where I want to take you with all of this baggage that you're carrying; I've got to purge you. Will you trust the process?"

Transition

Once you've been prepared, positioned and purged, you're now ready for the transition. When the children of Israel were about to transition into destiny, Joshua told them to "prepare provisions for themselves." In other words, get your supplies ready, don't wait until the last minute before you get everything in place. Get connected with the people you will need later now. Build the necessary relationships now because, in three days, you will cross over, so get ready for your transition.

God operates in time frames, and once God opens the door, you have got to be ready and prepared to walk through the door that he opens. Are you prepared to move? Are you ready to experience 'Better?' This is what you've been dreaming of; this is what you've been waiting for. This part, no one can do for you; you have to get up, take the necessary steps, and get your feet wet. Walk on the water.

We are told that the Jordan River they walked on is two hundred miles long, and the start of it is thirteen hundred feet above sea level, and by the time it dumps itself into the Dead Sea, it is eleven hundred feet below sea level. Throughout this process, it has twist and turns, ups and downs, just like life itself, so when it's your turn to transition, expect twist and turns, ups and downs. As you step in those waters by faith, the Lord will be with you as he was with Peter. Remember, God has already positioned, prepared and purged you of all that is necessary to get you to your destination. So, cross over and possess all that is yours. Better is Ahead.

"The only impossible journey, is the one you never begin."

TONY ROBBINS

17

Reaching the Other Side

That day when evening came, he said to his disciples, "Let us go over to the other side." Leaving the crowd behind, they took him along, just as he was, in the boat. There were also other boats with him. A furious squall came up, and the waves broke over the boat, so that it was nearly swamped. Jesus was in the stern, sleeping on a cushion. The disciples woke him and said to him, "Teacher, don't you care if we drown?" He got up, rebuked the wind and said to the waves, "Quiet! Be still!" Then the wind died down and it was completely calm.

(Mark 4:35-39 NIV)

One of the things I love to do in life is travel. When I get on that plane and take off, something happens to me; I feel like I'm leaving every problem and care behind. I'm smiling at everybody I meet. I'm polite to the grumpy; I even offer my help to passengers who try to retrieve their belongings from the flight's overhead compartments. I love that early stage of the journey. That beginning stage provides such expectation, thrill and joy, but I've also noticed time and time again that as the journey begins to exceed five hours or so, another thing happens. I start to get irritable, and the longer the journey goes on, the grumpier I get. I'm kind of embarrassed to admit that at this time, another sensation starts to overwhelm me. Frustration and impatience become visible, and I start wishing for the journey to be over. All I want to see at that point is the so-called "Other side" because it doesn't matter how beautiful the start of the journey is, journeying for too long always takes its toll.

This is the same with life because there are journeys and seasons that we go through that start with great joy and expectation. We are excited at first because we see great possibility and opportunity, but if the season that we are in or the journey we are on begins to drag on for too long, the experience starts to take a toll. Before long, the joy we had and the excitement we felt begins to fade. All we want to do is to make it to the other side.

A woman can tell you that the journey of pregnancy consists of three trimesters that produces similar emotions. I saw this so clearly when my wife was pregnant with my boys. Although each pregnancy was different, they all had similarities. They all started with great expectation, excitement and joy. We knew we had morning sickness to come; we knew we had sleepless nights to come, and we were even prepared for the swelling. I think I came out in sympathy because as my wife began to put the weight on, so did I.

The first few months are called the first trimester; this is the beginning of a pregnant woman's journey. It is indeed an exciting time but also a very delicate time. Although the woman may not look pregnant, her body is going through enormous changes as it accommodates a growing baby. This first trimester is crucial, for it is during this time that the baby will develop all of his organs; that's why a mother is told to maintain a healthy diet, to avoid smoking and cut back on drinking alcohol; however, this is just the beginning of the journey.

The second trimester is the most comfortable period for a woman. Most of the early symptoms gradually disappear; they feel a surge in energy levels and look pregnant. At this time, their appetite increases, and the weight gain accelerates—the time when it all starts to show. People begin to ask questions as the bump starts to get bigger and bigger. It is at this stage that we began to choose names.

By the third trimester, most of the developmental stage of the baby has occurred. He or she begins to grow in size, and travel is restricted. This stage of the journey brings real discomfort because the growth is rapid, and finding comfortable positions to sleep in is a challenge for any mother.

In the middle of this stage, all a woman wants to do is be on the other side of delivery so they can begin motherhood. Having travelled this journey with my wife three times, I can tell you that, what starts with excitement and expectation, ends with a longing for it to all be over. All we want to see and experience, is the baby that has been growing in the womb all this time.

The journey to wellness

In Mark 4:35, Jesus has been teaching a multitude, a crowd of people that had been surrounding him, pressing on him and grabbing at him since chapter two. Imagine an assembly of more than two thousand people all wanting a bit of you; things got so bad that Jesus told his disciples to get a boat ready so that he could make a quick exit. Later, he gets in the boat, moves away just a little bit from the shore, and continues teaching the multitude that has followed him to the seashore. When he had finished teaching them, he turned to the disciples and said, "Let us cross over to the other side." So, the destination was evident; however, the itinerary wasn't.

Not long after they begin the journey, the Bible says a storm arose. Winds started to push the boat; waves began to rock the boat, and water flooded the boat. Things got so bad that these disciples, some of whom were experienced fisherman, started to panic; that's when they began looking for Jesus, who was on the boat somewhere. They eventually found him in the stern of the boat sleeping on a pillow.

This confused them because they couldn't understand how Jesus could be in the middle of such a violent storm and be asleep. They woke him up and asked him, don't you feel the winds pushing the boat? Don't you feel the waves rocking the boat? Don't you feel the water in the boat? Jesus, don't you care that we are about to die? Jesus stood up, took a stretch and said two words in Greek, "Siōpaō Phimoō," which is translated as "Peace be still", but a more literal translation is, "To shut the mouth with a muzzle." When

Jesus spoke to the winds and waves with these words, immediately the storm ceased causing the disciples to ask themselves, "what kind of man is this, that even the winds and the waves obey him?" After rebuking the storm, Jesus turns and rebukes his disciples. Why would you be scared? Why would you panic? Are you telling me, all it takes is a little storm for you to start panicking in life; For a little contrary wind to blow against you for you to think you will die? and with this, Jesus begins to teach them another lesson.

Jesus addresses the fact they have allowed fear to overwhelm them. He addresses it because, during our journey of getting to where God has ordained for us to be, storms will arise. It doesn't matter what the storm is, be it a bad report from the doctor, news of being laid off from the job, bills dropping at your door, or somebody walking out on you, you cannot allow the storm to cause you to fear because fear and faith cannot operate in the same space. Fear has torment (1John 4:18), and when it torments you, it debilitates you. It stops you from being able to function and concentrate.

The Bible says: we walk by faith and not by sight, so no matter how the storm may appear, that is not how we are supposed to see it. An appropriate acronym for FEAR is "False Evidence Appearing Real." The enemy will bring things to your journey to make you so afraid, prevent you from crossing over to the place of destiny and success but remember fear is not of God.

This text shows that when journeying, there are some people and some things, you have to be willing to leave behind. Notice who Jesus left behind; he left the multitude, the people that were pressing Him and grabbing him, those who were slowing him down, those who only wanted something from Him but not Him. They were the ones He left behind. As well as people, perhaps there are some memories and hurts you have to be willing to leave behind too because the journey God has you on is not for everyone; not everybody is destined to journey with you.

Identify those things that need to be left behind. Perhaps it's a relationship that has no potential; it's going nowhere. Maybe it's a weight or a sinful habit that easily besets you, identify it and unloose it from your life; you've got somewhere to go.

When you continue reading the text, the Bible says that some other boats went with them, which means although some people and some things have to be left behind, there are a few that you need to take with you. It wasn't a lot of boats but just a few boats; you don't need a lot of people, only the right few people, those who will pray for you when you're weak, those who will encourage you when you're discouraged, those who will come alongside you when you are lonely. That's the beautiful thing about being connected with a church family; you have the right people with you.

Sometimes when I visit the sick in the hospital, I am saddened by the lack of visitors that some other patients have. Some of them don't have any. During that journey of sickness to health, you need people with you. Sometimes staff do not give the same level of care to those who lay by themselves, perhaps because they see they have no family members or friends there to check up on the care given, so they treat them differently. On many occasions, I have sat and talked with patients who lay alone, those who have no one visiting to offer some love and support, and it is always very much welcomed. Could this be what Jesus meant when he said these words:

> *For I was hungry and you gave Me food; I was thirsty and you gave Me drink; I was a stranger and you took Me in; 36 I was naked and you clothed Me; I was sick and you visited Me; I was in prison and you came to Me "Then the righteous will answer Him, saying, 'Lord, when did we see You hungry and feed You, or thirsty and give You drink? When did we see You a stranger and take You in, or naked and clothe You? Or when did we see You sick, or in prison, and come to You?' And the King will answer and say to them, 'Assuredly, I say to you, inasmuch as you did it to one of the least of these My brethren, you did it to Me.'*

(Matt. 25: 35-40 NKJV)

The others that were in the other boats were the ones who were part of the multitude, but when they saw Jesus get in his boat, they decided I'm going to get a boat too because I want more of Jesus; I want to be close to Jesus. When you choose your few, don't choose people based on how they look because looks fade and people change. Choose those who first and foremost want Jesus, those who love him as you do, those who will run after him with a passion, because they are the ones who will stay with you through the stormy journeys of life.

Notice that when the storm came, those boats didn't turn around and go back; they stayed. That's the kind of people you need in your life; anybody can stay when things are good and rosy, most will remain while the sun is still shining down on you, anybody can hang around whilst you have something to offer them. But you need people who will stay with you when all hell is breaking loose in the middle of your storm.

When the disciples woke Jesus, they said to Him, "Carest thou not that we perish?" By phrasing the question this way, they are implicating everybody, even Jesus, in this dilemma. They are saying Jesus, we all are perishing together. Can you imagine how ridiculous this must have sounded to Jesus? As if implying that Jesus came from heaven to earth, travelled through forty-two generations, to be born supernaturally through a virgin, only to come down to earth and die on a boat in the middle of the sea.

Jesus knew that he was going to the other side. There was no way a storm would stop him because He had a ministry to perform. On the other side, there would be a lame man sitting by the pool of Bethesda waiting to hear a command from Jesus to "get up, take up your bed and walk." On the other side, a woman with an issue of blood needed to touch the hem of his garment. On the other side, there was a cross on which he would later die for the sins of the entire world. Jesus knew he was going to the other side, and no storm sent by the devil was going to stop him because he had a purpose to fulfil. It was this primary lesson his disciples should have learned by now.

So, when the disciples spoke to Jesus, Jesus spoke to the storm. Jesus shows us that all you need is faith to be able to talk to your storm. Speak those things that are not as though they are. That's what the Bible tells us to do. We have been given the power to command with our words. Rebuke your wind and command your waves to cease and cross over into destiny. Better is ahead.

The importance of crossing over

They continue sailing, and the Bible says that when they made it over to the other side immediately as they disembark, a demon-possessed man ran up to Jesus and fell by his feet. This man was a sight to see. He lived in tombs; he was full of sores and cuts, as his habit was to cut himself with stones. Nobody was able to tame him because demonic forces controlled him.

As he threw himself on the ground, he cried out, "What have I to do with You, Jesus, Son of the Most-High God?" When Jesus asked the demon to identify himself, he replied, "my name is Legion for we are many." Jesus then gave the unclean spirits their marching orders, he told them to get out of the man. They begged Jesus, saying, "Send us into the swine, that we may enter them" because there were at least two thousand swine in the mountains. Jesus permitted them, and with that, they came out the man and entered the swine, causing the swine to run violently down the hill into the sea. These two thousand swine could not bear what this one man had been enduring for so long.

I'm hoping that by now you realise that the storm that they encountered on the sea was a demonic ploy to stop them from getting to the other side. Had Jesus and his disciples not crossed over, countless persons would not have been made better. On the other side, ministry awaited them. This man's life and many others depended on it. So, you must cross over; you must complete the journey you are currently on; somebody is waiting for you to impact their lives. You have been called to do it. I referred to this kind of success as "good success;" a success that impacts not only your life but also the lives of others. We are called to do this. We are called to be 'Better.'

"Death is not the end of life,
It is only the gateway to eternity."

18

Eternally Better

Lord remind me how brief my time on earth will be. Remind me that my days are numbered and that my life is fleeing away.

(Psalm 39:4 NTL)

Until now, we have spoken much about successes and things being better for us in this life, but it would be awfully remiss of me to simply talk about success here on earth and neglect to speak about the most critical success of all. Just as the nine-month spent in your mother's womb was preparing you for life here on earth, the life you live here on earth is preparing you for life in eternity. God has a purpose for your life on earth, but it doesn't end here; God offers more than just a lifetime opportunity. He has an opportunity that goes beyond this lifetime. The Psalmist sums this up with these words, "But His plans endure forever; His purposes last eternally. Happy is the nation whose God is the Lord; happy are the people he has chosen for his own! (Ps. 33:11-13).

God has chosen some people for his own, and they are the ones who open their hearts to him. He calls them 'The Elect.' Isn't it exciting to know that God's plan for His Elect involves far more than what we experience down here on earth? Life on earth is a temporary assignment; that's why the Bible describes earthly life as a mist, a breath and a runner. It's like we are just visitors travelling through. I've also read in the Bible our description as being pilgrims, foreigners, strangers and even aliens – you get the point. Therefore, our thoughts towards this life ought to be somewhat different from the world. They live and behave like they are going to be here forever, but we know our citizenship is in heaven and therefore, we must always live with that in mind.

The Bible says we are Christ's ambassadors (2 Cor. 5:20), which means we belong to another country, another system, another kingdom, we serve another King. If we begin adopting the values, lifestyles and customs of this world, along with its priorities, have we not then sadly compromised our ambassadorship? Have we not become traitors to our homeland? Perhaps we sometimes feel dissatisfaction and discontentment here on this earth because we need reminders that certain cravings and longings we have, this world simply will never be able to satisfy. The only way in which we will be genuinely be fulfilled is when we leave this place.

The famous songwriter Jim Reeves penned these words "This world is not my home, I'm just passing through, my treasures are laid up, somewhere beyond the blue, the angels beckon me from

Heaven's open door, and I can't feel at home in this world anymore."

The apostle Paul says something similar about our status here. "For we know that when this earthly tent we live in is taken down (that is when we die and leave this earthly body), we will have a house in heaven, an eternal body made for us by God himself and not by human hands" (2 Cor. 5:11). Here the apostle Paul reminds us that there is another life after this life, with another body made for that life. Most of you will be aware, especially if you have 40 in the rear-view mirror, that this body we are currently enjoying, now and then, gives us warning signs that make us know we are getting older. And no matter how we live in this body, it will wear out one day because we were not meant to live here on earth forever. If we measure our time here on earth against eternity, it is no more than a blink of an eye.

Life is short; eternity is long; even if we live for one hundred and thirty years here on earth, that is an unbelievably short amount of time compared to eternity. We were made to live forever; our spirit was made to last forever. This life is simply the practise workout before the actual game, or perhaps you could call it the dress rehearsal for the main event but whichever way you look at it, after we leave our life here on earth, we begin life somewhere else.

My father, Dr C T Wallace, would always say, "Something within me is crying, home sweet home." Although he loves life, he knows this is not all there is, that there is a much better-promised life ahead, and so he thinks about eternity often. There is much wisdom in doing that. Most people only think about eternity at funerals because they believe it is morbid to live life thinking about death, and I totally understand that view. Still, we shouldn't live in denial of what is inevitable either.

Because we know that this is not it, but that this is more a warmup lap before the main event, we should live our lives in preparation for the main event, for what is inevitable. Not too long ago, a slogan became rather popular, encouraging people to live each day like it was the first day of the rest of their life, and I understand the hope and excitement that slogan offers, it fills you with optimism, but the better advice would be to live each day like it was the last day of your life, that whilst you are living and living your life to the max, remember Solomon said, God has planted eternity in the human heart, but even so, people cannot see the whole scope of God's work from beginning to end (Eccl. 3:11).

Eternity for the believer

As I am writing this, I can hear somebody's thoughts loud and clear, "What is eternity going to be like?" Jesus said, "Do not let your hearts be troubled. Trust in God; trust also in me. In my Father's house are many rooms; if it were not so, I would have told you. I am going there to prepare a place for you. And if I go and prepare a place for you, I will come back and take you to be with me, that you also may be where I am" (emphasis mine).

> *"Everything that is not eternal is worthless in eternity."*
>
> C.S. LEWIS

Many verses in the Bible offer us a glimpse of what eternity will be like for the believers, but even these verses offer only a glimpse.

Our pea-size brains will never be able to fathom the greatness, splendour and joy of what is to come. Those pictures of people playing the harps and sitting around on clouds with halos are man's attempt to show heaven as a place of peace and serenity, but believe me, an eternity in heaven is so much more wonderful than that. Our limited imaginations could never stretch to visualise all the beauty God has prepared for us. The apostle Paul tells us in 1 Cor. 2:9, "Eye hath not seen, nor ear heard, neither have entered into the heart of man, the things which God hath prepared for them that love him." Simply put, we cannot even imagine the immeasurable greatest, and we will also be reunited with all our loved ones and friends that have gone on before.

I heard a story of a retiring missionary coming home to America on the same boat as the president of the United States. When they arrived, a cheering crowd came out to meet the president, a red carpet was laid out for him, the military band was playing his song, and the media came out and welcomed him home. The missionary, on the other hand, slipped off the ship without being noticed. There was no crowd there to greet him; no music played in his honour; there were no media paying attention to his arrival. They had not noticed him. He began praying to God whilst trying to deal with the self-pity and resentment that was overwhelming him, and as he complained to God. God gently reminded him, "My child, you are not home yet."

My brothers and sisters, when life gets tough, and it might; should you ever get to the point where you're tempted to throw the towel in because doubt has overwhelmed you and discouragement is speaking to you, remember that "You are not home yet;" when you get home, you will experience - Better.

Eternity for the unbeliever

Whilst we are offered many choices here on earth, eternity simply offers two, life with God or life without Him. Life in heaven or life in hell and what determines where we will spend eternity are the decisions we make here on earth now. There are many scriptures in the Bible that give us insight into hell and what it will be like, and all of them causes me to shudder. When I think about the gravity and the horror that those scriptures describe, it makes me wonder who in their right mind would consider choosing such a place?

Hell was created for the devil and his demons, but now sadly, it is also available to those who foolishly reject Christ. God said in Deuteronomy 30:19, "Today I have given you a choice between life and death, between blessings and curses. Now I call on heaven and earth to witness the choice you make. Oh, that you would choose life so that you and your descendants might live!"

We have all been given a choice, we can choose life, or we can choose death, and when we talk about death in eternity, it is not merely ceasing to exist, but this death is eternal separation from God. Can you even imagine a life where God is not present at all? That would be hell.

I overheard someone saying that when they die, they want to go to hell because that is where all their friends are going to be, that they are going to have one big party, but the only one who is going to be celebrating and partying in hell is the devil himself for having got you there. Hell, it is a very real place. Jesus says in Matthew

13:42, it is a place where there will be wailing and gnashing of teeth. A place of utter darkness "where their worm does not die, and the fire is not quenched" (Mark 9:48). And the worse thing of all is that hell is forever; whoever enters there abandons all hope. The horror of hell for even a second, is unbearable but forever, is more than unimaginable.

The answer to eternity

This kind of eternity though it exists, does not have to be your destination. Whilst we are still alive, we can make sure it is not. Rev. 20:15 tells us, "If anyone's name was not found written in the book of life, he was thrown into the lake of fire." God has a book full of names, names of the people who are destined to live with him in heaven. Here is the good news! There is a way to have your name written in the Lamb's book of life. It is the only way, and once your name is written there, hell will never be your eternal destination, and that is simply by accepting and living for the One who paid the penalty for your sins.

"Jesus in this life is everything you need for the next life."

Jesus says, "…. I came that they may have life, and may have it abundantly" (John 10:10). When Jesus came into this world, it was for one purpose, and that was to die on a cross to save humankind from their sin, and in doing that, saving us from hell too. When Jesus said, "It is finished," He took upon himself the punishment for sin so that we would never have to be bear such punishment ourselves. The apostle Paul tells us in Romans 5:22, "Therefore, having been justified by faith we have peace with God through our Lord Jesus Christ."

This word justified means "to be declared righteous." Jesus made it possible for us to be declared righteous and at the same time giving us peace with God, so now not only can we have peace with God but also the peace of God. We no longer have to try to justify the crazy things we have done; we have been justified – declared righteous. Now all you need to do to ensure that you spend your eternity in heaven with God and not in hell with Satan is to invite Jesus into your life and let him be your Lord and Saviour, repent of your sins and allow God to forgive you and he will wash all of your sins away. Once you have Christ in your life, your eternity is secure. The greatest thing you can achieve in this life is the guarantee of knowing where you are heading in the next life.

Before I close this book, I want to offer you that guarantee. Once you accept Jesus in your life, eternity becomes a thing you can look forward to. Will you pray this prayer and receive the Lord into your life? Say it with me.

Father, in the name of Jesus, I recognise that I'm a sinner and need a Saviour. I believe Jesus to be the Son of God and that He came and died to save me from my sins and that he rose again that I might be justified and saved. Today, I repent of my sins, and I invite you, Jesus, into my life to be my Lord and Saviour. I give you my life, and from this moment on, I belong to you, Amen.

If you prayed that prayer and meant it from your heart, then allow me to welcome you into the family of God. You may not be able to see them right now, but angels are rejoicing because of the decision you just made. You are now a citizen of heaven with a guarantee that will never expire. Your name is now written in the Lamb's book of life. Please share this good news with somebody and find a Bible-believing church where you can share fellowship with other believers and worship the true and living God. My friend, if I never get to meet you here on earth, I will meet you one day in eternity. Better is Ahead.

Printed in Great Britain
by Amazon